Astrid Fox is the pseudonym of a literary novelist. We'll call her Ms X. But an additional alter ego has published the only erotic novel ever to feature Neanderthal hybridism and consensual cannibalism (*Primal Skin*, under the name Leona Benkt Rhys). Astrid a.k.a. Leona a.k.a. Ms X is a big fan of the cartoonist Steve Bell. That's her bedtime reading. She hopes this collection will be yours.

The Fox Tales

ASTRID FOX

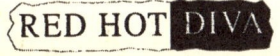

ALSO BY ASTRID FOX

Rika's Jewel
Primal Skin (under the name Leona Benkt Rhys)
Cheap Trick
Snow Blonde

The following stories have been previously published: 'The Devil is a Squirrel', *Best Bisexual Women's Erotica*, Cleis Press 2002; 'Frozen Violets', *Wicked Words*, Black Lace, 1999, under the name Leona Rhys; 'Lifer', *Viscera*, Venusorvixen Press 2000; 'The Missionary Position', *The Mammoth Book of Lesbian Erotica*, Robinson 2000; 'My New Boyfriend', *Libida.com* 2000; 'Sci-fi Cliché #10', *Wicked Words 5*, Black Lace 2001; 'scratch'; *Wicked Words 4*, Black Lace 2001; 'Sweet Poison', *Sugar & Spice 2*, Black Lace 1998, under the name Leona Rhys; 'Virgin Club', *Threesome*, Red Hot Diva 2002.

All characters in this novel are fictitious and any resemblance to real persons, living or dead, is purely coincidental.

First published 2002 by Red Hot Diva/Diva Books,
an imprint of Millivres Prowler Limited
Spectrum House, 32–34 Gordon House Road, London NW5 1LP
www.divamag.co.uk

Copyright © 2002 Astrid Fox
'The Case of the Cameo Rabbit' (short story) Copyright © 2002 Astrid Fox & Dr Stùpido

Astrid Fox has asserted her right to be identified as the author of this work in accordance with the Copyright, Designs and Patents Act 1988

A catalogue record for this book is available from the British Library

ISBN 1-873741-79-0

All rights reserved. No part of this book may be reproduced, stored in a retrieval system, or transmitted, in any form or by any means, including mechanical, electronic, photocopying, recording or otherwise, without the prior written permission of the publishers.

Printed and bound in Finland by WS Bookwell

Distributed in the UK and Europe by Airlift Book Company,
8 The Arena, Mollison Avenue,
Enfield, Middlesex EN3 7NJ
Telephone: 020 8804 0400
Distributed in North America by Consortium,
1045 Westgate Drive, St Paul, MN 55114-1065
Telephone: 1 800 283 3572
Distributed in Australia by Bulldog Books,
PO Box 300, Beaconsfield, NSW 2014

CONTENTS

Introduction   vii

Lifer	1
scratch	9
My New Boyfriend	29
The Devil is a Squirrel	35
Angelica	49
Nugget Nancy, Queen of the Yukon	59
Allure	79
Sweet Poison	85
Frozen Violets	97
The Curie Quandary	113
Sci-fi Cliché #10	119
Reds	137
Sister Six	155
Serpents, Corn and Honey	163
The Case of the Cameo Rabbit	181
The Missionary Position	209
The Werfox	215
Virgin Club	225

*for Venetia,
one kick-ass
fairy-tale princess*

Introduction

These are for the most part fairy tales, even the science fiction and fantastical ones. Many are spiced with a wicked pinch of Scandinavian mythology, including 'Sweet Poison'. This was the first short story I ever wrote and the first thing I ever had published, erotic or otherwise. I even self-plagiarised a paragraph from the literary novel I was writing at the time. Others are more recent, such as 'The Devil is a Squirrel' and 'Reds', both of which were penned in the spring of 2001. 'Reds' is a hybrid of three fairy tales, actually: Rapunzel, Rumpelstiltskin and O Henry's 'Gift of the Magi'.

Other pieces in this collection are semi-historical fiction, such as 'scratch' (Vikings again), 'Nugget Nancy, Queen of the Yukon', 'The Curie Quandary' and 'Serpents, Corn and Honey'. In one of these, perhaps not the one you'd expect, you'll find the intrepid Rika, a character from my first erotic novel *Rika's Jewel*. And you'll have to humour me with the dyke erotica/detective pastiche 'The Case of the Cameo Rabbit', co-written with the formidable Dr Stùpido. A girl can only churn out so much sex-drenched prose before she wants to satirise it; think of it as light reading after all that smut!

I've always had quite an anarchic attitude when it comes to the writing of erotic short stories and have written, for money and fun, whatever tickled my fancy. But when I reviewed this collection, I realised that fully twelve of eighteen stories involved some form of rebellion. And rebellious people, as well as those who play with other people's expectations, are people I've always considered very sexy. Sometimes, for women, the simple fact of acknowledging that we *have* desires is rebellious. So let's hear it for the girl who follows her own clit and values her own pleasure; for effete men and boyish women; for smart blondes, lesbian nuns and Gold Rush whores; for the grown-up versions of Huck Finn and Pippi Longstocking; for Eve, Prometheus, Xena, Jesus Christ, Lucifer, Comandanta Susana, Rani Sahib Kaur, Hildegard von Bingen and Peaches. Because nothing's sexier than a rebel with a cause.

Astrid Fox, October 2002

Lifer

Lifer

People say I'm a pretty woman. They look at my clear complexion, my glittering green eyes, my beauty-queen-blonde hair and blow-job lips and they say, there goes a pretty woman. Of course, it helps that I'm married – that little gold band is a social prophylactic. People feel safe letching. They want to fuck me. But I'm off-limits.
Off-limits.
Sometimes the lesbians want me too, not just the men. I watch them ogle me. They can't help it, they're different to us, you see. They want women just like men want women. You can never really trust a lesbian, you know, or be close friends or anything, because there's always that little thought in the back of your mind, isn't there, that some day, some moment, they might turn and make a pass. Like men, there's only one thing on their mind. Just like that lesbian over there. I saw her the first second I walked in the visiting room and I knew what her game was right away.

Prison visiting rooms make me nervous. They're so dirty – okay, not really dirty, but depressing. Scrubbed clean but full of dashed anticipation, old arguments still hanging around in the air, sealed lust. Vulgar plastic chairs, suspicious stains on the screen, the whole lot. I guess it's because I don't belong in here. But she does, that lesbian, that dyke over there. She does. She looks like a lifer. Just look at her.

I glance around the room, but there's only the two of us in here, separated by a flat sheet of clear plastic. I'm still standing by the door, though. Safer that way. They used to use glass for the screens, but you can imagine what happened then. I can already feel her watching me, her eyes sweeping over my cleavage, her butch hands tightening at her sides. She wants me. They're all the same.

I figure what the hell, and I meet her eyes. There's nothing wrong with flirting a little, I guess. I raise my hand to my bright-red lips and flick my tongue over my wedding ring, just so she sees. It's never been removed or lost and it's true, I feel grateful for the privilege that keeps this small hoop around my finger. Yes, a social prophylactic. Safe. The gold feels ice-cold on my tongue and now it gets cool and wet and shiny. Her eyes flash suddenly, and I realise I'm flirting with danger. She runs her hand back over her short, spiky hair and we end up staring at each other for half a minute. I can feel my heart pumping wildly away. I'm not sure why.

'Ms Allen, is that your visitor?' Someone comes into the room, their voice full of raspy authority. The dyke heads towards the partitioned chairs and sprawls down on hers, smirking through the plastic, as if to say, well?

I look behind me. The attendant is bored and doesn't care anyway. I slowly walk forward and then sit myself carefully down in the chair opposite the dyke. I can't believe I'm doing this. The smell of prison is in the air: depression, despair, arousal. I can feel myself go wet. Maybe just this once.

I raise my lashes. She's there on the other side of the transparent screen, everything my mother ever warned me about. Lifer. Prison-bent. The words come back to me again; they're haunting my consciousness. She has tattoos up and down her arms. Her eyes are black and sparkling; her hair is dark brown. I think she's Chinese. I think she's around thirty. I'm sure she's a dyke. My mouth has gone dry. I don't usually do this sort of thing. I feel myself begin to blush. I'm starting not to feel like a lady anymore, but more like a – well, like a slut. A slut for a lesbian. How low can you go. I touch the ring on my left hand with my right index finger. There's an ache between my legs. The attendant is still not paying any attention to us; she's reading some prison brochure that they hand out to families for coping purposes.

The dyke is staring at me arrogantly. And then she makes a crude gesture at me, with her tongue and hand. A *really* crude gesture. I can't believe it. A slash of pink tongue wiggling sleazily between fingers. That's what this type of an environment does to a person. But I'm also starting to feel hot, like my skin beneath my dress is bursting out in prickly heat. The ache between my legs hasn't gotten any better. My cunt feels slippery.

The normal question is rearing up its ugly head up, you know the one: what does a girl do to get in here in the first place? But I've decided I've got no time for questions like that. Slowly, I raise one leg up, one foot on the chair as I push my hips up, still sitting. The dyke's eyes barely glimmer, but I know what she's seeing and I know how the sight of my red wet pussy will affect her. Split-beaver. Men, women – they're all the same.

The dyke makes the same coarse gesture, and now I can tell that behind her impassive expression she's turned on, in pain from lust. She's just barely in control. She motions for me to touch myself, and the signal is a raw one. I can feel my blood singing in my veins now, and somehow I've gotten myself in this weird head-space where it's true, all I really want to do is masturbate before this big butch dyke, my fingers sticky in my pussy.

Her eyes gleam as I hitch my skirt up even further, exposing even more of myself to her, my hand rubbing all over my hot snatch. My palm and wrist are soaked; I'm that wet. I spread my legs wide on the chair and rub my pussy wet into the cheap plastic upholstery. I just spread my cunt juice all over that chair. And

I look over at her there, at her utility wear, at the keychain tracing her hip from pocket to belt-loop. Just look at her. She belongs here. Here, in a dangerous place. I start to roll my fingers over my stiff clit. From the corner of my eye, I can tell that the attendant's still not paying attention. Or maybe she's enjoying the show. Who knows. Who cares. I don't.

All I want to do is rub my fingers fast and hard over my clit. I know how juicy I look; I know how abandon is already creeping its way over my face. My breath coming quickly, my pussy drenched and creamy and red for the butch dyke across the screen from me. I pull down my neckline so that my tits rise up full and plump, my stiff nipples just out of sight beneath the tight fabric. *You like that?* I think at her. *You like Mama's tits pushed up so you can take a nice long letch?* I can still taste the raspberry-flavoured lipstick I applied earlier, right before I entered the room. She's leaning forward now too, her own rough hands down her trousers, touching herself; trying to get a good look at me through the glass. All the same. Filthy-minded. She's mouthing something at me through the screen, but there's a roar in my ears and I can't even make out her words. So I make them up for her instead: *you want it like a bad girl wants it*, she's saying to me, *flat on your back with your pretty ass in the air, waiting for the wicked witch straight out of a 50s porno mag to come at you with a slap.* I can smell sex in the air.

The scent of cunt just crosses right on through that old plastic screen. She's stopped saying whatever she was trying to say, her eyes screwed shut, sweat gathering under her arms, her dark hair shining, her fingers just circling and circling and circling in her pants. For me. For the type of girl she can't get. I know what she's thinking now, too. She's thinking I'm a bad girl. *A bad girl. Breathing Betty Page dreams into my pillow at night.* Something dark is rising up in my mind and it smells – *like whores and jizz; it's wicked and it's bad and you're nothing but a slut.* She's furtively wanking, her hand down deep into her hairy pussy. Filthy.

Lifer

Filthy-minded. Like me. Like this place. It's full of forbidden danger, I think, as I push down hard on my clit, my breasts jiggling; I'm so wet and now I don't care whether the attendant's watching or not, all I want to do is come. My hair is damp and I'm beginning to feel pleasure spiking up through my fingers from my cunt. I can barely see the dyke now, my vision's gone all blurry, but I get the impression that she's wanking quickly, too. I'm full of lust and so is she. I bite my bottom lip until it bleeds. Fuck, I think, fuck, I'm so horny; so horny, and my mind is full of danger, bad-girl dreams. Dark and terrible and I'm wet like blood; I'm tasting blood in my mouth and I know this goes far deeper than smiling Betty Page; this is the same dark taste as XXX and it's the twisted sexuality of the girls they flash up at you in those serial killer films I hate to watch and it's bad stuff, nasty, so bad, raspberry lipstick and blood and as I come the whole chair is wet with juice; and I'm there, still panting, my vision still flashing black to red to black, my hand still trembling over my cunt. My bleached blonde hair is damp against my neck as I stare into the dyke's dark eyes and as I observe her flushed cheeks.

She came, too.

'Ms Allen,' the voice comes without warning, 'your visiting time is up.'

They're going to take her away. I push my skirt over my hips. The dyke smiles at me, almost wistfully, as she's escorted out respectfully, even if she is drenched in the smell of sex. She chats with her escort and they laugh together; it's a good idea to remain on friendly terms with the screws if you want a blind eye turned on the next visiting day. And I – well, I am trussed again, my hands cuffed behind my back, the metal scraping lightly on my ring, and I am led back to my cell block, which is where I'll wait until the next visiting day.

scratch

scratch

Imagine, if you will, a tree. A tree more enormous than the world itself, a tree which itself holds the earth within its scope. The green sweeps of the tree's branches arch out from its trunk like plumage, and the jade-blushed feathers of the leaves are impenetrable and thick, exposing little of the undergrowth. But among the depths of these same leaves and along these same branches stride various creatures, initially familiar but strangely equal in size: a stag nibbling at leaves, a huge squirrel poised on a hidden limb, a vast glittering hawk whose wingspan takes in the breadth of a thousand villages. Beast and fowl alike might be colossal, but they are also dwarfed in the great green cloud of the mythic tree's foliage. Below its dense greenery the trunk curves down, a huge astral trunk of crumbling bark and layer upon layer of new growth, dead wood, new growth, dead wood... The tree shifts, changes, retreats: the process is endless; the tree is eternal.

Down goes the trunk, down through the constellations and the firmaments, past the gods' abode, all the way down to the world itself, set high above the roots of this Yggdrasil Tree, roots whose base is still watered by the tears of three crones. Yes, the world itself is set high: a world of ice-bright seas and lands of blood and soil, of stench and sex, and a world bound tight by the coils of a great serpent, whose constricting hold squeezes and shakes the very seas on which the priestess's boat now topples, a hold that jars and shudders the invading Viking ship in a shower of foam and dirty brine. With salt-water clogging her throat, the priestess prays to the Red Thor to stop the storm, to ease his hammer between the snake's tight spirals, spirals held fast by daggers of its own teeth. With her knife, she scratches a rune into the oak of the ship. At last, there is success. Her words and her carved invocation coax the worm's great fangs to loosen, and all is calm again.

The men are grateful, but no one speaks to the priestess for the next few days of the journey.

They sail for another three and a half days and when they reach the coast the stink from the vessel is terrible. But clear skies hasten the last leg of the journey into the island, and spirits are high. Adrenalin is in the air, too, as the sailors morph into warriors ready to pillage, rape and burn.

The men have avoided the priestess, as much as they have been able to in a cramped ship where a person can scarcely take a breath without inhaling someone's beard. Still, she has kept to herself down by the far end of the prow, and apart from making the usual enquiries as to weather and luck of the battle, the men too have tried their best to keep their distance.

She is a strange woman, and there is no denying that. She admits it herself. The priestess Veleda enjoys her reputation.

*

In this Year of Our Lord 793, the young monk Cuthbert guards over the incorrupt body of the Sainted Cuthbert, after whom he has been named. His hands riddle over a rosary made of the small white rocks the sea spews up. Each of these stones looks like a bone-hard tiny sea-creature. Each resembles the Holy Rood itself, each is a little crucifix bead spat out from the sea that surrounds the Holy Island. Already pilgrims take the stones away after they

scratch

have visited the incorrupted body which young Cuthbert tends, already the stones are known as Cuthbert's Beads, after the Saint whose name this seventeen-year-old has the privilege of using.

In this summer month of June, there have been flashes across the heavens of Lindisfarne, great streaming lights across the sky, portents of fire and dragons and trauma. The other monks on the Holy Island are uneasy in the evenings as they whisper to each other after vespers, but throughout the early summer while the other brothers worry, young Cuthbert sneaks off to his cell and strokes himself with pleasure, the comets roaring outside the groove of his window while his fist is on his cock, and he strokes and pulls and gasps and thinks of evil flesh, of men and women, of the smell of his own juice in his hand. He licks his lips, eases his hand along his cock and dreams of soft bodies and hard sinews. Then the pulse comes, and he shudders with a terrible enjoyment; he grunts in satisfaction then cries out as his sin shoots out of his cock, into his fist, liquid and sexual. The comets still tear through the twilight heavens, and Cuthbert hopes then that the other monks have not overheard his efforts.

He knows these self-ministrations are wrong. He knows these thoughts and actions both are evil.

*

The fighting has quieted, and Cuthbert still waits in his hiding place in the cellar where he has been sobbing silently since darkness fell. He has heard the slaughter above, and he has caught just a glimpse of the yellow-bearded warriors who had landed their boats on the shore and then attacked with such force. The smell of smoke indicates that they might have set fire to the living quarters, and they have taken all the holy icons and gold from the church where he now is hiding, but by some miracle have left the holiest item of the monastery untouched: the incorrupt body of the Saint.

In his cellar, young Cuthbert spits. These pagans cannot see the true value of sanctity; they see only the glitter of silver and gold; they do not see God's worth. But then Cuthbert censors himself: of course, it is a blessing that the pagans did not take the abbey's most valuable treasure. There is Our Lord's hand in this, somehow.

Though not young Cuthbert's, because his hand was elsewhere; he had done nothing to prevent the ransacking of the chapel. Instead he had watched through a crack in the cellar beneath the shrine as the filthy warriors had laughed at the Saint's body, when they had seen it was only a corpse, and one of them had even reached up and shoved it. Most had seemed hesitant to touch it further, however, and Cuthbert had seen through the crack how the blasphemers had busied themselves with the gathering of silver chalices and golden plates and pewter candlesticks instead, and his heart had boiled in wrath. And then, worst of all, Cuthbert had watched as he saw a female heathen come forth from amongst all the filthy savages, a sorceress of some sort, and saw how she marked the wooden base of the holy shrine itself with a knife, making some sort of devil's symbol, which Cuthbert, because of the angle of his hiding place, could not make out. A female, a most evil Eve, in God's own house, defiling the shrine of a saint!

And now Cuthbert shivers in the cellar in which he has hidden since the attack, for he had been attending to his own dirty lusts in his cell when he heard the first shouts, and had just spent himself in a profane orgasm when, in a surge of deep guilt, he had left his living chamber and had run to the chapel which held the Saint's body over which he was supposed to be keeping watch; he had run like a coward and then, after he had sneaked by the butchery, seeing how the other monks had been slain or bound as slaves, he had crept below the church by an old tunnel he had once discovered, and there it was that he had witnessed the great plunder of God's own riches. Now Cuthbert closes his eyes and shudders. That someone could steal from God Himself! What particular penalties of

scratch

Gehenna await these murderers, he cannot imagine. Surely a worse hell than the normal one, for the theft of God's possessions is far worse than the theft of those of mere mortals!

Still, Cuthbert cannot at the moment fathom a hell worse than the situation in which he now finds himself. Brother Abelard was slain as well as Brother Joseph, and young Brother Jonas, whom Cuthbert had always secretly admired, had been bound up by rope with twenty or so of the other monks, heading towards some evil heathen slavery...

But now Cuthbert's breath catches, because he sees the sorceress entering the chapel once more. Anger swills up in him as he watches her light the candles of the church, candles which have been discarded on the ground after their holders were stolen. The sorceress pays no attention to protocol, so she does not care that the wax will now drip and tarnish the holy floor; she rights the pale-blue candles and anoints them with fire anyway, so that soon the whole church is glowing with flame. But it is wrong, so wrong, Cuthbert thinks, because what wicked heathen ritual will now be performed?

Because there is some terrible devil's magic at work here, because though Cuthbert should hate the very sight of the Jezebel, instead he discovers that he does not – worse, the sight of her inflames him with the very passion that is his secret guilt every evening in his cell. Her flaxen hair seems air-light and sensuous, her lips seem to moisten even as he stares at them, and there is the evil flush of sorcery to her cheeks and her bosom, a flush that makes his chest grow tight. Beneath his robes, he is stiffening at the sight of her. And now, as she bends over to light another candle, a slim tapered candle blue as the sky itself, he can see the sway and jiggle of her unbound breasts, promising a Satan's lushness of silky skin, promising the satiny feel of carnal satisfaction with another human that Cuthbert himself has never yet experienced. Cuthbert's mouth has gone dry, and his heart is pounding.

Astrid Fox

With a stick dipped in God knows what substance, the sorceress marks a symbol on the floor of the chapel, and this time Cuthbert can make out the stick-like figure. It is no symbol with which he is familiar. He begins to shake. She has lit what seems like a hundred candles, and there is a hellish glow in the chapel now. Cuthbert has never been more frightened in his life.

Yet also, his blood is rushing through his veins, making his cock rigid and urgent with need. He runs his fingers over the white beads of his rosary strung round his neck, but his hands are shaking – he wants to touch himself, but to touch himself in this profane way, under these profane circumstances, under the very shrine of Saint Cuthbert, is surely a mortal sin. Perhaps it would be justified if in some way he could match the profanity of the spell the northern whore now was weaving. He could desecrate her religion, and by his action then redeem his own.

Candlelight floods in through the crack in the floor of the chapel and quietly, quietly, Cuthbert scratches out a replication of the sorceress's symbol in the dirt with his index finger, upturning the rich dark loam of the cellar so that the rune stands out in relief like a brand. He moves feverishly, his hand cramping, desperate now to fufil the invocation, to tarnish the sorceress's own spell. But now he is too full of his own need; he grips his hand round his cock and pushes his fist up and down on himself, as desperate to come as he is desperate to finish this spell of desecration. It is the Jezebel's fault; it is this sun-haired Jezebel who has tempted him like a succubus, tempted him in her whorish manner with her heathen magic.

He feels dirty and unclean, as dirty as a woman, as a shameful daughter of Eve, and it makes him masturbate harder, poison and lust swilling up to the tip of his cock. He has to rid himself of sin. He has to force it out. He looks through the crack at her wet, sly lips and her long white throat and he screws his eyes shut. He wants to come all over that throat, spew over it in a rain of sinful, hot seed. He can feel lust rushing through him now, tight and

scratch

urgent, like an itch. The whore. The – sluttish – vixen. How – dare – she – tempt – him – like – that. In his mind, he sees her neck and chest covered with his emissions and this makes him even harder, and he jerks more forcefully at his cock.

'Deliver me, O my Lord,' he prays, as the evidence of his temptation bursts out onto the ground in a cool white spurt, over the devil's rune that he had torn into the ground with his own fingernails. And what does it matter? Let sin lie with sin. He feels better, now. Clean. Purified. Deep in the cellar, under the altar, young Cuthbert sighs and kicks dirt over the rune, as if he'd never drawn it at all.

*

The warriors have done their work, and now it is up to Veleda the priestess to ensure the continued success of the raid, for these warriors have never come across such easy pickings before. Not only was the settlement rich beyond dreams, with treasures to be melted down in a molten sea of silver and gold that would shame a dwarf but, amazingly, the defenders of the settlement, though all male, had put up no resistance at all – had not even been trained, apparently, in the simplest art of self-defense. Really, they had only themselves to blame. And now, while her countrymen drink their toasts to a future of many similar raids, it is Veleda's task to purify this stinking church of stone and twigs where the islanders conduct their primitive religious ceremonies, for her countrymen have insisted that the exposed body is in itself a *draugr*, the most unholy of all undead spirits in the form of a living corpse, and it is up to the resident priestess to render the curse of a *draugr* unable to affect the luck of the invaders.

So Veleda puts on her robes, tries to block out the events of the evening – the killing and enslavement were necessary, of course, but not to her own taste – and begins to light the candles that are littered round the dank chapel.

It is good that she does this, because as soon as the chapel is illuminated it becomes a far less fearful place, and Veleda is able to see quite clearly that the body that lies on the shrine is not that of a *draugr* at all, but only a dead man, albeit a well-preserved dead man. She wonders for a moment why he has been attended to with such ceremony, but then dismisses her musings: who knows how the minds of such people work – with their odd little all-male cult on an island off the coast of this foreign land. They no doubt worship death itself, not life, if she is to judge by the decorated walls of the building in which she finds herself – for many of these illustrations depict a pale man hoisted up by his wrists on some type of a frame, with his feet nailed fast, and if he is not meant to be dead, then he is certainly meant to be seriously ill. To Veleda, this is distasteful: she worships life itself, however short or long it might be, and she knows she is only capable of understanding a cosmology such as her own people's – a sacredness of living things like the Great Tree itself. Anything else seems pointless – even abhorrent. Perhaps the men of this settlement all deserve to be killed, after all, so that they do not spread their death-worship even further. As she lights the last of the candles, Veleda thinks of the White Christ missionaries which had visited her country so unsuccessfully, and a frown crosses her brow. The men of this island are of the same type, she thinks.

But now she stands, holy in the middle of the building, and feels herself surrounded by light, by fire itself, and it clears her thoughts. She feels calm for the first time since the long sea journey – she often wishes it were not necessary for there to be a priestess aboard each raiding party, but the raiding sailors insist on it, for luck – and she closes her eyes and lets the candlelight flicker behind the shutters of her eyelids. Her body, too, relaxes, and her heart slows, and she knows that even if it is not a *draugr* that sleeps there on that platform of wood that she had marked earlier, well, it will soothe her mind and flesh to let herself go once more into the peace of meditation.

So she stands there for a while, eyes closed, and feels the whole power of the Tree flow through her, feels life itself pour out into the church through the channel that is her body, feels the excitement of life-force flicker through veins, out through her fingertips, out through the soles of her bare feet, and then she knows it is now time for the final step of the ritual: it is time to mark the environment with a rune.

Her heart is beating quickly once again as she brings forth the charcoaled stick from her robes; she feels strangely light, excited, aroused. The marking of the rune is always a moment of anticipation, and her body reacts accordingly. She slides her fingers beneath her robe and over her breasts, pinching at her nipples, then removes her hands so that she can write the rune.

She still has no idea which rune shall be revealed to her.

She stands there in the middle of the foreign cult-place, candles flickering around her like many stars, and feels something like a wind rush through her: again she feels full of the life-force; she is driven to write down the rune the Tree has given her. She scratches it out on the stone floor of the church with the charcoaled tip of the stick.

It is a surprise to her: the lines she has drawn spell out the N-rune – *naudr*, need. But I have no present needs, thinks Veleda, I am at the moment quite content, except perhaps for the pleasurable ache in my groin, but that is the usual result of the ceremony.

She stares at the symbol *naudr*, her breath coming quickly.

Then she hears what sounds like a sigh from where the corpse is lying, and at first her blood chills, but then there is another sound underneath it – a scurrying, like that of mice or rats. She knows she is hearing another human, and for some inexplicable reason she now feels *naudr* throughout her body – she needs to fuck, and she will fuck whoever is there, be it a spying countryman – who should know better than to peer in on one of her rites

– or a withered male inhabitant of this defenseless but rich settlement.

'Come out!' she commands, but there is silence. The need of the rune courses through her, its magic and its desires, and she repeats herself. Then she takes out her knife and catches the candlelight on it, so that any spy might see that she is indeed a threat and will do well to obey. She has no fear of her countryman warriors, strong though they are, for they are too frightened of her power and they need her services and advice for the sea-voyage home.

But again there is no response.

Veleda walks closer to the altar. There, she sees a crack in the raised floor, and a pale eye staring up at her. She puts her knife down to the crack and shows the eye its blade. 'Come up now,' she says, 'come out from your hiding place.' She knows that even if her tongue is not understood, her meaning is implicit.

Now there is a stirring, and it sounds like a movement below the very stone floor she stands on, and then out from behind one of the pillars there creeps a young man.

In fact he is a very young man, a boy of sixteen or seventeen, perhaps. He has rust-coloured hair and a freckled complexion, though his hair is shaved round his skull. He wears a long brown robe of simple woven material, and around his neck is a string of white beads, which he is clutching in both hands. Compared to her countrymen, he looks effeminate and weak, as if the blood he spilled would be as pale as milk. He looks pious.

And amazingly, he smells of sex. And Veleda, who is well versed at reading faces, can discern that, through the terror evidenced upon his visage, there is also a trace of guilt. She glances down, and sees a dampness evident groin-high on his robes. And she realises that he might have been hiding in terror, but his hands have not been idle, not at all. And as she stares at his crotch, she watches as the swelling there once again begins to emerge.

scratch

Ah, the resilience of the young.

Immediately, she wants to bed him. Veleda wants to train those adolescent hands of his to stroke her body; she wants his lips pressed to her anus hot and tight, licking her until she squirms. Already she can see how his breath quickens when he looks at her; how his gaze falters, but then how he tries to sneak a look at her breasts under half-closed lids, for her robe had fallen open earlier when she herself stroked at her cherry-red nipples. Veleda wonders whether this young man has ever seen a naked woman.

Yes, her own land had had the missionaries of this man's ineffectual White Christ before, and Veleda had heard tell of the White Christ's hatred of flesh and pleasure, but this young man seemed to be no stranger to self-pleasuring, even in the midst of a raid.

Veleda feels *naudr* run through her body and she grabs the necklace of the young man and with it pulls him towards her, though in doing so the string breaks, and the beads fall to the floor. The boy doesn't flinch, however, though it is plain that he is aroused, and he stares Veleda in the eye with something like hate. This irritates Veleda. She is a priestess of life, after all, not a stripling of some order that worships death. She stares him back in the eye, perhaps only a hand's breadth between their two faces, and says, 'I am Veleda. I am a priestess – you are merely an acolyte, of some effeminate cult that can't even bring itself to bear arms. I am Veleda,' she repeats, pointing to herself.

The boy glares back at her, and then he draws back several paces and mutters something that sounds like 'Cuthbert', a hideously harsh sound of a name, and he points to himself, before glancing quickly up at the corpse above them with something that looks like shame. But Veleda doesn't care about the boy's motives – he has disturbed her ritual, and now he is going to help her complete it.

She points to the charcoal rune. '*Naudr*,' she says.

The boy – Cuthbert? – looks at the rune and spits on it.

Veleda strides up to him and grabs his jaw. He is still glaring at her, but he has also positioned himself so that he is surreptitiously running his fingers against the side of her bosom, as if he thinks she will not notice. She slaps his hand away, and then pushes him down to the floor. He leers at her – has he no shame? – and then, worse, strokes the bulge of his erection through the cloth. He mutters something at her again, and for Veleda, this is the final insult.

She tears off her robe, and watches the boy's eyes grow wide at the sight of her breasts, her tapered waist and the fine, full blonde bush of her sex. She motions for him to remove his clothing and, to her surprise, he does so, with no mutterings and with more respect than he exhibited only moments before. Veleda shoves her hand in her pussy until it is wet with fluid and then holds her hand a finger away from the boy's nose. His anger seems to have dissipated away, as is surely typical with men of his weak stock. He sighs, and closes his eyes. Veleda takes the occasion to pause and run her gaze over his body, and she finds it entirely to her liking. Then he sticks out his tongue and licks her juices away from her proferred hand, inhaling her scent with obvious relish, and Veleda understands from his eagerness and clumsiness that he is, indeed, a virgin and that somehow this was why the Tree had offered forth the N-rune of Need, for it is her need, too, that fills her with desire and makes her thighs sticky with want, even now. For most of her countrypeople are too frightened of her power to approach her with sexual intention.

The young man who calls himself Cuthbert lies back on the floor, passive in his inexperience but still eager as a puppy, lapping and kissing her hand and wrist like a true sensualist, not like a flesh-hater at all. Veleda first resolves to be gentler, but then she kisses him hard, and soon his tongue and mouth are as ardent and even as violent as hers, biting and nipping and probing her lips, like a man dying for water, such is the young man's thirst for erotic sensation. So Veleda indulges herself in sensation as well, and her nails scratch his back in pleasure. Then she raises herself and steps back for a moment to observe him. He is an avid student, despite his initial anger for her, which she supposes was understandable under the terms of the raid.

The candlelight laps around the two of them on the stone floor, the sticks of blue wax shining across the entire church. Then Veleda sees the white beads, spilled onto the floor from the force of her initial tug on the string round Cuthbert's neck. She gathers up several in her palm, six or seven of them.

Cuthbert is leaning back on his palms, watching with interest. He also looks fearful, as if she were doing something quite forbidden.

Veleda does not break his gaze and she pushes one after another of the beads up inside her pussy, beads which have no particular importance to her but beads which no doubt are filled with some terribly important meaning for young Cuthbert. Her fingers grows sticky with the task, and once more she allows Cuthbert to lick at her hand, a favour for which he seems very grateful.

Then she stretches her naked body down on the cold stone beside him, and guides his mouth to her sex, so that he can continue his licking there, and she feels soft tremors start to flow, and she swivels so that her own bright lips are fastened tight on his cock, which is so urgent that already a drop of moistness appears at its tip. She sucks that moistness away, and is rewarded with a soft whimper from Cuthbert himself.

Veleda can feel him licking out each of the little beads she has pushed up inside herself, and she thinks of the blasphemy he must feel as his tongue curls into her heady juice. With his mouth, he strokes out each little marked bauble. Veleda's own mouth goes dry, then she feels herself relax into the slow eroticism of the act, and finds herself enjoying the thought of his young pink tongue moving slowly over the slippery lips of her sex, drinking her. His prick in her mouth becomes harder and more urgent as he licks and licks at her, slurping and swallowing and she slides into pleasure even as she sucks even more violently on his stiff cock. Then young Cuthbert draws his cock away from her lips, his cock with its musky animal scent that inflames her, the scent and flavour that makes her just want to suck and suck and suck.

Cuthbert's fingers enter her cunt, and seek out the last of the little beads. He speaks now, pointing to each X-mark on each bead, beads which he seems to consider sacred, but the words he says – 'crucifix', 'rood', 'cross' – are words which Veleda has never heard before. He draws back so that Veleda can watch him put each into his mouth, her juices mixing with his saliva, her juices corrupting his flesh-hating religion, and this thought makes her burn with even more desire. Her nipples are tight as rocks themselves, her thighs are quivering, her powerful, sticky come is in his mouth.

She stretches her arms out towards him, wants to feel those tender ribs of his, his delicate, cloud-pale buttocks, his ribs beneath his skin, the hot yet tender flesh of his prick. Cuthbert sighs, and puts his hands on her waist, and pulls her on top of him with the confidence of movement from a more experienced man than he is, so that Veleda straddles him and he groans with pleasure. And Veleda, well, Veleda feels the thickness of his cock impale her, as she slides down on him, her cunt tight and moist, for she is dripping liquid, she is so wet she feels as if she were melting into a lake, but here in the lake's middle is a source, his cock, that plunges up inside her and fills her with an itching lust, a need to push down further and further on him.

He moans with her movements.

It fills Veleda with a thrill that she is fucking this boy for the first time, that he is moaning from the pure pleasure of sensation, not the removed fantasies of sex that fill the heads of those more experienced. He wants her, not an idea of her. And he wants the gritty satisfaction she is giving him, as she grinds her hips down. She can see it on his face when she looks down through half-drawn

scratch

lids, can see the wonder in his eyes and his slack, open mouth. Now she shoves herself down on him with force, and he give a soft groan and a whimper and stiffens even more inside her. Veleda falls down on him, whilst still moving her hips, so that the pressure on them both is not alleviated. She feels wanton as she nips at his tiny nipples, pale as his lips, bites the taut young skin on his upper arms. She smells his underarms and sticks her tongue into these crevices and licks at his downy fur that she finds, and this sends a pulse all the way down to her cunt, a long string of desire from her wet mouth to the pounding drumbeat of the bead of her sex. As she inhales the scent of his excitement and sweat, he begins a long drawn-out moan and starts to thrust his hips upwards rhythmically, pulsing with a climax he can't long restrain.

Veleda is so aroused by his lack of control, his unconscious moaning, his inability to do anything else but rock his hips towards his own pleasure that she too begins to moan and flush and rock back and forth, so conscious of his stiffness rock-hard inside her, and her hand rubs out a complementary rhythm, sticky and frantic over her own small stiffness. His cock. Her fingers. His innocent face. His tongue snaking out to lick at his lips still smeared with her own juices.

*

After their pleasure, they lie there for a while on the stone on the warm June night, Cuthbert's fingers playing idly with Veleda's pussy, and she lets him insert and remove his fingers in her wetness until she grows a bit bored with the game. When their breath has returned back to them, Veleda gets up and walks to the entrance of the church. She looks outside and sees that her countrymen have congregated down on the beach, where they are drinking. From where the church stands, Veleda can see all the way down to the other side of the island as well, where there are several abandoned boats, and so she beckons Cuthbert towards her and motions to him that he might at this moment make a clean escape while the backs of the Viking men are turned.

As Veleda quickly helps him don his robes again, she smiles. For there, scratched in red relief onto Cuthbert's back in the course of their passion, is a large invocation of the *naudr* rune. May he never forget or dismiss the pleasures of the need of flesh again, despite the teachings of his faith. She hopes it will be a lesson he remembers. It was the least she could do for the sake of his life-force, for the sake of the eternal green sap of the Tree that runs through us all.

*

Cuthbert is full of wonderment and fear as he rows his way swiftly to the mainland. And once there, he will seek out those who will help him recover the Saint's body. It has been a night of both delight and trauma. When he looks up across the lap of the waters, he sees his own abbey, full of flickering light, and he mourns for those slain and for the future of the souls of those brothers of his who have been spared, at the heathen hands of such strange monsters as these invaders. And yet there is still a resonance in his groin when he thinks of the pleasure the sorceress has just shown him. Surely these must be the delights of Eve against which he has been warned, and rightly so, it seems, for surely the taste of the sorceress's sex is like the fruit of Eden itself, the one forbidden fruit. His arms ache and yet it is his whole body that is flooded with the memory of her flesh. Though perhaps there is hope for her? She was not unkind to him; perhaps Our Lord will see fit to save her soul. Was not Magdalene herself spared? Cuthbert sighs and feels himself hardening again, even as his arms pull the last stretch towards the mainland. He has himself made a small attempt, in any case – he left one of the crucifix-marked rosary beads

scratch

behind in the wicked flower of her sex, so that the message of Christ might flourish even there, even there in the very source of tempting sin itself. He thinks of the small white bead lavished with her juices, and his groin tightens. Though he concentrates on his rowing, instead. He tells himself it was a selfless act. It was the least he could do for the good of her soul.

My New Boyfriend

My New Boyfriend

My new boyfriend's thing is lesbians. He told me this just this morning, while we were in the shower together. Just as my hand had worked up a nice slow rhythm on his cock, his eyes popped open, and he said: 'Tina, have you ever thought about doing it with another woman?'

I didn't answer him right away – I let him lean back against the shower tiles, his chest still nice and soapy, me still stroking away at his cock until he was ready to burst, nearly ready to come, and then I leaned even closer. The water was getting in my eyes and I pressed my tits against him and felt him go even stiffer. I gripped the hot flesh of his prick and I said, 'Yes.' And he came right then, his semen spraying warm and silky, all over my hand. It made me so wet.

The fact is, I lied. It's not that I have anything against lesbians. It's just that it's not my thing. It doesn't turn me on. But Joshua was in a hurry to get to wrestling practice after our shower, so I didn't get a chance to tell him the truth and wasn't sure I wanted to anyway.

I clocked Joshua's tight ass in his new Twister jeans as he headed out the door, all intent and serious for his sport. He has a fine body with broadish shoulders on a slim frame with just enough muscles to keep a girl very happy, if you know what I mean. That's the thing, see: I'm into men. I like their slick taut abdomens and that furrow of hair that just goes down, down, down to a thick cock and the fuzzy hair covering a pair of nice firm balls. I like the scent of fresh male sweat. I like young men squirming with testosterone who bust out in hard-ons if you just happen to smile at them the right, sleazy way. I like men. So sue me.

I guess this is why I've always gone for athletes – not jocks, mind you: *athletes*. There's something about a guy's body all pumped up with adrenalin and perspiration that really gets me dripping. My clit just clicks into overdrive. I've dated runners, bicyclists, swimmers, hockey players and a basketball player. When I went out with Stephen, who was semi-pro, he was so tall I was dwarfed beside him: a tiny specimen even at five-foot-six, all long brown hair and big brown eyes. When we held hands, he looked like a big brother taking his favourite kid sister to the game. But you should have seen Stephen on the court with all those other men: moving together like a ballet, competing, working up a sweat. It was something else.

Joshua, as I said, is a wrestler. He has a match on tonight, matter of fact, and I can't wait. If I think too much about it, I'll get too horny, and then I'll have to rub myself all wet and slick, and then I'd have nothing to look forward to. So it's better this way, doing what I'm doing. Being patient. Waiting.

The match is even more exciting than I had hoped for. I'm on my own in the bleachers, my ass pressed into the wood, squeezing my thighs together. I'm licking my lips like an old pervert, hungry for the sight of all that young male flesh. There are other girlfriends here, all sitting together, but I don't want to sit with them and cheer *en masse*. I want to have my thoughts for myself. I know it must look a little strange, a young woman sitting all by herself, watching her boyfriend so intently, not rousing the team with all the ex-cheerleaders over there. But I have other things to rouse

My New Boyfriend

myself with. Where is Joshua? The smell of men is rising all the way up from those hot, sticky mats. The gymnasium feels too hot.

It's his weight class. Here he is now, the blue outfit delineating his nipples on his lush dark skin, his skin already perspiring from the heat. And here is Jake, his opponent. Jake is much fairer than Joshua: blond, pale, almost as lovely in his own way as Joshua is.

Their bodies start to move against each other; pushing and thrusting, skin skimming skin; my mouth is beginning to water. I wonder if the other watching girlfriends are thinking the same thoughts that I am. I see Joshua's hands gliding over Jake's pale chest: it's strength, sure, but it's sex too. There's no way you can't call this sex. They are fighting each other and grunting. Joshua's nipples are like dark little stars; sweat is already beading down his chest: making him shiny, beautiful, glowing. I imagine Jake licking it off, then reaching down to my new boyfriend's prick and jerking him off quickly, leaving him breathless. I can even taste Joshua's come at the moment, and I imagine Jake swallowing it down, Joshua's cock pulsing in his throat, Joshua's eyes closed tight as he leans back and lets the other man suck him dry.

I open my eyes: I'm still on the wooden bleachers. Embarrassingly, my hand has found its way to my crotch and I'm rubbing myself, right here and now. I hope no one has noticed. But no, people are cheering: Jake has won. I feel bad for Joshua, but I'll also take pleasure in consoling him, later this evening. Maybe I can waylay him tonight before he steps into the locker room, maybe get a chance to slip into an empty corridor and fuck him before he takes a shower, while he's still smelling of both Jake's sweaty body and his own.

Later that night, he asks me the question again: 'Do you like the thought of two women together? Do you get off on the idea of homosexual sex?'

Astrid Fox

'Sort of,' I say.

'Sort of?'

It's only a half-lie, isn't it? There's another match on tomorrow night, and he'll be wrestling Jake again. I'll tell him the truth after the match tomorrow. I promise.

The Devil is a Squirrel

The Devil is a Squirrel

The devil's not so bad in the sack, you know.

She's not. Not if she tries, anyway. She can get a little lazy, what with her hot 'n' horny reputation and all. But let's face it, things tend to go her way: the filthiest and most satisfying curses, the most delectable transgressions, the moistest chocolate cake, and plus she's got all the best songs.

It's not like she doesn't care about sex. Oh, she does. Maybe the devil may care a little too much, and then POOF! – look what happens – she gets her fingers burned, and then she just figures, why bother next time, so she doesn't, 'cause why make the effort?

It can happen to the worst of us.

It even happened to me.

Okay, the truth is, it never happened to the devil. I lied about that. She has always enjoyed a whole lot of loving. But the bit about her not being so bad in the sack – well, that bit is true.

I met the devil last August in a grimy, Hell's Kitchen section of East London – my neighbourhood, actually. It being London, and also being the wettest English year on record since records began in 1776, it was raining.

I was in a bad mood last August. I had had it with polyfidelity, monogamy and particularly with celibacy. As a result of the disastrous consequences of the two former conditions, I had been practicing the latter for a good few years. Six years, six months and six days, to be precise. By choice, obviously. Obviously, by choice. I made a conscious decision to value my sexual self and change my non-sexual-self-respecting life by making different conclusions the next time around. So obviously, it was by choice.

It always is, right? *Right*? So stop snickering. I hadn't been laid since February 9th, 1994. Last summer, the middle of post-millennial August should have been a swelteringly hot, steamy, sunny day, yet I was drenched in the middle of Hackney. I was miserably soaked. Miserably soaked and shagless is a terrible condition in which to exist. I had gotten way past any concept of blue balls – or blue labia, I guess – many years before.

What's the matter, haven't any of you ever had a dry spell before?

I was having a dry spell in the middle of England's wettest spell ever. There was irony in there somewhere, but by that point in time I was far, far too bitter to care.

I was taking a short cut home, my jacket pulled up over my head, since I had lost my umbrella on the underground on the way in to work. I was mumbling something about the stupid, cursed, bloody weather and stupid, cursed, bloody fellow pedestrians who insisted on walking where I wanted to walk and stupid, cursed, bloody cars splashing through stupid, cursed, bloody puddles; mumbling how the devil could take them all, because I'd had it, absolutely had it: with life, with London, with my perpetual paucity of shags, and how I'd be damned if I was going to spend yet another year with a big fat zero on the action front. I think you know what I mean.

I dodged the traffic at last and cut through an alley, trying to remember, with some irritation, whether or not I had anything in the freezer to pop in the microwave for dinner.

And that's the point when someone hissed at me from the deepest corner of the alley.

'Psst! Come in here!'

The Devil is a Squirrel

Without my umbrella, rain was dripping down my neck. The alley had the semblance of shelter, thanks to a green awning overhead.

'Just a little closer.'

I could barely see. I took a moment to wipe the rain out of my eyes and began to make her out more clearly. She appeared to be unarmed. She also looked out of place in the gritty dinge of a trash-covered alley. I say 'she' casually, as if the devil were any other female. Let me tell you, she wasn't. Long, sleek dark hair. It looked liquid: like molasses, like treacle, like honey poisoned with ink. She had a knock-out body, too – even asexual little ol' me could see that. Curve to curve to curve. Like a glam-o-rama starlet: really stacked. I think you know what I mean. Said curves were swathed in what looked to be a strapless taffeta frock, circa 1959. It was blue as a prom queen's eyes, but in this dress the dark-eyed woman put all predictable prom queens to shame. I think you know what I mean. So: 1) dark hair, 2) sinful eyes and 3) a to-die-for body in a killer dress. Murder by numbers. (But, see, I hadn't clocked onto the fact that she was the devil yet, you know?)

She smiled at me.

Even then, not knowing what she was, I wanted her to have some effect on me. I wanted her to make my pussy wet and my clit hard, but she didn't. Female impotence is a very weird thing.

'Come in a little closer,' she requested.

Listen, I didn't want to get stabbed. I stayed where I was.

'Suit yourself.' She lit a cigarette. She stared me out. 'Well?'

'What do you mean, "well"?'

'Hey lady, you're the one who called me up. Now why don't you cut the crap and we can get started?'

'Excuse me?' I was staring with horrified fascination at her as she took exactly three steps towards me. Her hips swayed provocatively. Her cleavage shifted appreciably. Just watching her made my mouth dry, the way you feel when you're watching an especially good theatrical performance. But it didn't make me wet. In fact, it made me annoyed, because when she sashayed up to me and stuck her tits in my face, she blew a purposeful mist of cigarette smoke straight into my eyes.

Her eyes were narrow and glittering. There was a flush to her sallow skin, as if she were particularly excited about something.

I thought about taking a step back. There was only one advantage to staying here in the alley, and that was the fact that it was shielded in part from the rain. The disadvantage, of course, was a possibly imminent mugging.

She didn't move away. 'I don't have a lot of spare time, sister. What's it going to be? Coffee, tea or me?' She pushed her breasts against my own – quite brazenly, I have to say.

I knew it was a proposition, but I hadn't had one in so long – well, at least not one from anyone who wasn't four sheets to the wind – that I have to tell you, I was a little shocked.

I asked myself what she saw in me: cranky-looking woman of about forty, short hair, glasses, fairly butch (but looked like she could swing for the home team, too, in a rough-and-rugged kind of way). I didn't look straight, gay *or* bi, if you really want to know. I was the original female eunuch. More than anything else, I looked grumpy. Which I was.

Maybe she was drunk, after all.

'Hey!' She snapped her fingers near my ear, which is something that always pisses me off. 'I mean it. Make your choice – chicks, dicks, combinations thereof, or the red-hot mama herself, yours truly, *au naturel*.'

I tried to regain some composure, and cleared my throat. 'And who might "yours truly" be, then?'

At last she took a step back, and then she burst out laughing.

'You're great!' she said, not very nicely. 'You really don't get it, do you?'

The Devil is a Squirrel

'I'm afraid I don't. Thanks for the invitation and all that, but I'm just going to have to make my way home now, put my frozen dinner in my microwave, settle down and –'

'Shut up, yeah? Take a look at me. Come on, take a good look.' She stood back and did a twirl before posing, rather sarcastically, with her hand on her hip.

I sighed. And then reckoned that the sooner I humoured her, the sooner I'd be on my way. So I took a good look this time.

Okay, to be fair, she had a hell of an aura, what with that snug dress and with her dark hair tossed back as if she were Jessica-fucking-Rabbit. A sinister aura. In fact, you could say she *glowed* with malice and ill intent. If I had been the susceptible type, I might even have called it allure. Her smirk, her blood-dark nail polish, her lush wicked body – it was like the air around her was sizzling and crackling. I thought back to what she said about me 'calling her up'. I thought back to my cavalier cursing at the London weather and my current nun-like state – the six years, six months and six days since last I shagged. I wasn't a specialist in the proper cataloguing of medieval court records and witch trials for nothing. I got it.

I wasn't particularly shocked. I guess that, just as my senses were dulled to sensual pleasure, so was I also impervious to full-scale, supernatural shock. After so long without any sort of stimulation, carnal or otherwise, I was just kind of floating along in a celibately grumpy haze. Nothing really got to me anymore. Not even this.

'Thanks, but no thanks,' I said. 'I'm sure you're perfectly delightful, but historically I think there's a downside to playing with fire, if I remember correctly. Loss of eternal soul and all that...' My voice trailed off. I was staring at her cleavage, her tits being thrust up by some invisible but terribly effective support system. There was a sheen to her skin. I didn't think it was rain, but just the faintest layer of perspiration. I wondered how hot her skin was on this cold rainy day. I watched a tiny drop of sweat trickle down between her breasts. For the first time in many years, I felt a dim jolt of desire, a little twinge between my legs.

I cleared my throat hurriedly. 'Anyway,' I continued awkwardly, 'I have to get home.'

I found that I was still staring at her tits.

Jesus. How exactly *does* one go about turning down the devil?

She moved in on me so that she was within a couple of inches, once again. Let me just say this: she was very quick to take advantage of any weakness.

'If you don't mind my saying so,' she said in an irritatingly sultry voice, 'despite the weather, you look a little dry.'

'Excuse me.'

'A little dried up. Like a prune. Am I right? Okay, you're no spinster, but let's just say it's fairly evident you haven't had it for a while.'

'I beg your pardon?'

'A good long while, I'd say, actually. You're aching for it, aren't you? I bet it feels a lot longer than six and a half years.' She abruptly changed the subject. 'What's your line of work?'

'I'm a librarian.'

'A *librarian*? Please. No surprises there.'

'You can talk – look at the colour you're wearing. Talk about predictable. How about a little subtlety?'

'How about a little appreciation?'

In a suddenly crude motion, she hiked up her hemline and stuck her fingers between her legs. I couldn't see exactly what she was doing, but it was such a vulgar thing to do that a kick of desire jumpstarted my cunt. The feeling tightened and got worse. She withdrew her left hand with an audibly slurpy sound and raised her fingers to her mouth, smelling them and then slowly licking the juices off them, like the cheapest tart in town.

Her more discreet machinations hadn't worked, but this obscene

The Devil is a Squirrel

little display had my clit buzzing like her tongue was already working away at it. It was downright embarrassing. She'd worked out exactly what would get me going, and then did it. I felt uncomfortable – didn't want to be played like a fucking piano. But now I was horny too. Her dark, crimson, full lips made me wonder what her pussy lips looked like; I found myself straining my neck to get a look at the shape of her ass with its plump, high cheeks. Jesus, I felt like I were melting in her heat already. I almost didn't care.

I closed my eyes for a second, trembling, trying to get a grip on my sanity. It was highly unlikely that I was standing in an alley being propositioned by the devil herself. Maybe lack of nooky had finally driven me round the bend. Maybe one of those cars that had been skidding around on the wet pavement had crashed into me and killed me, and now I was in... heaven? Hell? Who knew?! I screwed my eyes tightly shut, trying desperately to think. I'd open them, and everything would be fine. I'd open them and I'd be alone in the alley and then I'd go back to my safe, celibate life.

'Maybe girls aren't your thing? I'm flexible, you know.' Her voice was very low and very sultry. I snapped my eyes open.

The bitch was really fucking with my head now. It was becoming harder and harder to convince myself I was sane. Because Temptress No. 1 had disappeared and Tempter No. 2 was in fine form. I do mean fine form. I don't fuck men all that often – well, up to six and a half years ago I didn't fuck men all that often – but in the good old days I was always open to suggestions. I was never completely closed off. If you know what I mean.

A certain type of tall, gangly, academic, smooth-faced, shy and cerebral boy could always make me go weak at the knees. One with disconcertingly sleazy eyes behind his specs that would belie his mild-mannered appearance, and make me wonder what perverse thoughts he entertained during the long hours spent studying in the university library. A few of those boys had passed through my own doors of knowledge in the past.

If you know what I bloody well mean.

The young man smiling down at me in the alley had *exactly* that look.

Yes, he was smiling, just as she had been, but he didn't have her smirk – his lips were curving politely; unlike her, he seemed passive, waiting for my move. He reminded me just a tad of my first boyfriend, Owen, from when I was fifteen. The biggest difference was that I had known Owen in the seventies and Tempter No. 2 was obviously from our present new century. He had long blond hair tied back in a ponytail and wearing a scuzzy black heavy-metal T-shirt – 'Queens of the Paleolithic' (or something like that; I don't keep up much with modern music) – and a pair of loose blue corduroy pants. Blue was a constant theme, I saw.

He was observing me carefully, respectfully. He still reminded me of Owen, and all of a sudden I had a flashback to the long hours my first boyfriend and I used to while away, making out until I was as wet as the weather today. My crotch soaked through my tight faded jeans, his hand tensed on a nipple beneath my halter top, his teenage hard-on thick and hard as rock beneath his flaring trousers; the obligatory plastic comb squeezed in tight against his young ass...

I could nearly smell Owen now, could remember the taste of his mouth and the way his kisses made my heart beat fast. The way I would stroke him until he groaned and came in my fist. The way his hand would glisten, sticky from finger-fucking me in the back seat of my parents' car. Then how we'd kiss again, after everything sweet had happened. Everything was always easy, smooth and sexy, smooth as butter, smooth as cream, smooth as fucking itself, and then we'd start all over again...

The devil's eyes were clever and knowing. The devil was as innocent as my very first fuck. The devil knew that, deep in my celibate, asexual skull, I could still remember things like that. I could still remember sex. And yet this devil was presenting me with an

The Devil is a Squirrel

older version of Owen, maybe a university, twenty-something version, not innocent anymore but still eager, young but aware.

He'd learned a few things. There'd been a few Mrs Robinsons around to instruct him. He was partial to older women, maybe. Maybe he even fancied grumpy old me. The devil knew damn well what he was doing. He pulled me toward him and we kissed. His tongue slid in my mouth quick and tight; his tongue tasted of cheap cigarettes and micro-brewed beer, like a college student's tongue should taste. I clung to him. I could feel the heavy push of his cock against my abdomen; I wanted to squeeze my pussy down on him, soft, wet and hot, and just rock and rock.

No! I swung myself away from him, breathless this time. The submission wasn't worth it: a shag for a soul. I don't think so, buddy. No matter how cute and pretty you are, or how many times you'll whisper Chaucer in my ear in the late mornings when you're prone to skipping class.

'You're a hard nut to crack,' the devil observed. This time his eyes were neither slow nor sweet. He gave me a once-over with that sleazy gaze, and I remembered all those late-twenty-something Ph.D. boys whom I observed so impassively week after week in my library.

Had I secretly wanted to fuck them all along, and just been unaware of it? Was the devil giving me the kind of man who would finger my asshole on a public bus, daring me to let on to the folk in the seats up ahead? Would he bind my wrists up and just fuck me, use me like a hole, while he selfishly pumped his cock away into my soft, sticky centre until he, and not I, had enough?

Would I beg him to slap me, and then watch his expression when I whimpered down on my knees? Whimpered in lust mixed with dark mind-fuck shame mixed with the twist of pain, wondering if maybe he enjoyed the crack on my cheek just a little too much?

I was doing it again. The devil was toying with me. He, she, whoever – it wasn't going to get me. The devil might know me inside out, but there was still free choice. My clit was as hard as Owen's teenage cock had ever been. My cunt was wet with desire. When I closed my eyes, I saw the devil's figure: a being with marvellous luscious tits that were flushed with want. Fantastic tits, with stiff thick nipples of candy-red; tits that made my clit twitch just at the thought; and beneath those breasts a smooth abdomen, and beneath the abdomen a thick long cock already glittering with wetness, as if it had just been withdrawn from a sopping pussy.

The devil had it all. I had to resist.

'I'm sorry,' I whispered, 'but no.'

The devil sounded ever so faintly amused. 'There's not a lot of options left, you know. Still, if you insist...'

Suddenly, instead of a grungey post-graduate student standing before me, there was a fluffy, bushy-tailed squirrel with bright black eyes. Its tail, I noticed, was blue. It looked like an exotic form of feather duster. Thankfully, the squirrel caused my desire to drain swiftly away. I was going to be all right.

I was going to be in control.

'I don't know where you get your information from,' I told the small rodent, feeling pretty stupid about it, too, 'but animals really aren't my thing.'

'I know,' said the squirrel in a mid-range voice – said the *squirrel*! Now I knew things were dire – 'I just wanted to illustrate an old German dialectal saying.'

'And what's that? "Don't head down trees head first"?' I asked. I was starting to feel like myself again, though lust was still resonating in little twinges throughout my body.

'"The devil is a squirrel", yeah? That's the saying I'm referring to. It means that sometimes odd things show up where you least expect them. I personally feel – and granted, I'm biased – that the

The Devil is a Squirrel

trick is to take advantage of odd opportunities whenever you can.' The squirrel's intonation rose on the last word, and the original dark-haired woman was standing before me, smoothing down her blue dress rather demurely.

It was good that she was human, but of course that meant that desire left me dry-mouthed and shaking all over again. All I wanted to do was fuck her. It was as if all the stored-up, unacted-upon desires of the last six and a half years hit me all at once and all I could think of was fucking and all I could see was fucking and all, at last, all I wanted to do was to start fucking.

It would be worth the price.

A good fuck would always be worth the price of an eternal soul.

For a second I hesitated. I had the weird feeling that there was a little struggle going on over my head, maybe between a tiny demon and a tiny angel on each of my shoulders, as in a Donald Duck cartoon. Maybe it wasn't a struggle. Maybe it was a negotiation. Maybe I didn't give a rat's ass.

'Oh, hang it.' And at last I stepped toward her.

So I fucked the devil. I fucked her as a girl. Or rather, she fucked me: three fingers up my wet cunt, with me bent over at the waist, nearly kissing the ground, my sensible librarian trousers bunched around my ankles. Her fingers were as gentle as ramming rods, as tender as a butcher's. These fingers of hers were red-hot pokers sliding into my slit – they would have felt bad, except they felt so good that I just gritted my teeth, tightened my cunt round her rough, hot hand and came like a house on fire. I mean, speak of the devil.

I fucked her as a boy. His mouth sucking and licking my pussy as his finger slyly intruded my asshole. His face shiny with my juice, until I pushed him on his back and rode him. His cock was thick and stiff inside me; the rain sparkling in his lashes was a nice grace note to his smooth scholarly ass rasping against the alley pavement. His hand tickled out a climax from my clit until the sensation was heavy, intense, crude. Until I would have sold my soul if I were forced to hold out any longer. Until I came, actually.

And I fucked her as a very tasty hermaphrodite: lips round the devil's cock, hand up the devil's snatch. Lovely. Let me tell you – something wicked this way came. Mmm.

I also fucked the devil in her previously referred to *au naturel* shape, and no, I'm not telling you what that was. I will say, though, that it made my head spin, literally. Have you ever seen *The Exorcist*?

Still, all in all the devil's an innately selfish person and therefore a bit of a pillow queen, so toward the end of that wet summer day she got a little lazy. Even that didn't stop me from enjoying every second – a soul's only a soul, after all. It's much better to have fun while you can. I haven't seen her since that occasion. I have spent the ensuing days since last August seducing and being seduced by mere mortals, and now I have to wonder why I ever stopped.

But even though that was last summer, today I realised something rather interesting. I have one over on the devil – a technicality, really: 'I'd be damned if I was going to spend yet another year with a big fat zero on the action front' – you see, the fine print, the wording. The thing was, I wasn't damned, because I did get shagged, and that was all down to the devil. Credit given where credit is due.

I figure she knew this. The devil's pretty experienced when it comes to contractual agreements. So why'd she do it? Was it a pity fuck? Did the devil have a sentimental turn of heart on the 15th of August, 2000? It was a holy day of obligation, after all.

Who knows? Weird things can happen. Fish can fly. Once in a blue moon, and all that.

The devil is a squirrel, yeah?

Angelica

Angelica

The glen had many trees with leaves that glowed. That's right, amongst the waxy greenery was phosphorescence; one leaf in three pulsed with the soft light of 1950s clocks.

The nun knelt there below the trees. Her eyes were closed, so she did not see the lightning bugs that bobbed up and down amongst the already glowing foliage; did not see that everything was rinsed with a tender green light except for her in her dark dress, dark stockings and brown leather shoes. Her order did not insist on habits, anyway; they were thought unmodern.

It was a special place where she knelt, but no longer a holy place. In the second decade of the previous century, three children had claimed that the Virgin had appeared to them here and for a year or so this little glen had been a pilgrimage, until the children, one by one, had admitted that they were lying, and no one came here anymore, mainly out of embarrassment.

An altar that had been placed here during that long-ago first year of excitement was still present, though, and it was here at the foot of four stone steps that led up to the former shrine where the nun knelt and prayed. She knelt the difficult way, straight up from the bend of her knees, rather than resting back on her haunches.

It was not just the leaves and the insects that emitted light in the glen, for she had lit a series of tea lights which framed the shrine and the steps. When the light was uneven behind her closed lids, she attributed this unsteadiness to these small candles, for they were notorious flickerers. The truth was, however, that it was the fireflies buzzing by silently within inches of her face.

These airborne insects were refugees from a genetic modifying lab some four or five miles away, and because of the harshness of their captivity they had been taught to fly quietly.

What did the nun pray for?

Here is how her prayer went, or rather how her prayer dissolved back into pondering thought, as prayers so often do:

Dear God, dear Virgin or whoever you might be,

Excuse me if I insult you by that address, but if I weren't honest about my doubts in your existence then you'd surely know. Yesterday Celia and I were discovered by Mary. It was just a kiss, and not our first, but it was such a sweet kiss, too, and in my heart I know that something so good and right can never be a sin. I know you know this as well. But Mary reported it, and Celia told Mother Wilgefortis that it was I who had initiated it. Celia took all that purity and sensuality, God, and she soiled it with denial. I am trying to forgive her, but I feel rage, not only that I will be disciplined for Particular Friendships, but rage at someone who only yesterday made me feel happiness, the soar of real emotion, God, the real true light of your Son and my Lord. No matter what happens, I will not deny this as Celia did, and no matter what pattern of frail and flawed human repercussions follow, I will continue to believe that you are truth, and light, and love.

This was where the prayer portion of her mind stopped, because then she knelt there on the hard stone and kept thinking of what Mother Superior had shouted at her about Noah's Ark and the pairings of opposites; and she also kept thinking, though, that such pairings would only be matched like bookends if the gender was the same instead of differing; and therefore Mother Superior had got it all wrong after all, particularly since Mother Wilgefortis always said *'Like attracts like,'* over and over again like a blasted litany. Even if she were asked to move to a different order, the nun decided she wouldn't care.

And her eyes flipped open then from sheer anger, and she felt it in her chest, but she had come to this quiet place for peace, after all, not wrath. She could still hear Mother Wilgefortis in her head: *'Adam and Eve, not Anna and Eve; Noah's Ark, not Gay Day in the Park,'* and she could hear her own voice arguing back, *'But Mother, you also say "like attracts like".'*

The lightning bugs were everywhere. She gasped just once and then held out a hand to touch one and it landed on her index finger like a butterfly, though she had never heard of lightning bugs doing anything as social as that. Perhaps they were some new variety. For that matter, she had never heard of lightning bugs in this area of the country, either.

Above her, the trees swayed slightly with the wind and she saw how their very leaves glowed, one leaf in three. It was like the lights at Christmas, but here it was not ornamentation but the actual leaves of the tree that shone, rather like those fiberoptic plastic plants she had once seen in a store window.

Oh, it was quite lovely. Then she looked down at herself and saw that her finger was turning white with light where the lightning bug had landed, and the glow was working its way inward to her whole body, finger then back of hand then wrist then three-quarters of her arm glowing now, the prettiest infection she had ever seen.

She did not feel especially surprised. It had been a long day, and the fantastical does not shock a tired mind as it does a well-rested one. Instead she watched with pleasure until her arm entire was glowing, and then her neck, and then she felt heat rush to her face and she knew it must be glowing, too. The white light slid down her other arm, and down her breasts and ribcage and abdomen and groin, and the whole sensation made her feel warm and tight and full of love. The wave of light reached the tip of her toes and stopped, and left her flesh illuminated like the small plastic statues they used to sell of the Virgin in the 1970s, statues which glowed green-white and faded with the hours of darkness to mere muted plastic by dawn, when you didn't need the Virgin watching over you anymore.

She looked up. Yes, she felt warm and fat and tight, like she had drunk a huge mug of glow-in-the-dark cocoa, or the same way she had felt on all parts of her skin after she and Celia had kissed the first time two weeks ago, right after morning prayers.

'*Adam and Eve, not Anna and Eve. Noah's Ark, not Gay Day in the Park.*'

'*But Mother, you also say "like attracts like".*'

She stretched out her hands and they shimmered like the tree leaves, and the lightning bugs moved with her in a little dance, and she felt she was travelling with them as they swirled silently around her head; as if she and the bugs were working together in the magic of shine, though their species were different.

She took all her clothes off then. How could she not? It felt right, there in the little green glen with the moon shining, and the trees glowing ghostly, and the insects, and the tea lights; and she laughed with delight when she saw how smooth the glow was from her breasts, and now the tight muscles of her bare arms glittered with movement. And her bottom; she turned around to see it, too, and it glowed perfectly there, a fine sheen to it that made her haunches look quite attractive, in her opinion. She hoped only that it would not rain, for then she would get cold.

While she was checking out the shine off her bottom, someone coughed near the altar.

She took her time turning around, not feeling particularly frightened because if she could glow like this then, if it was someone dangerous like a rapist or a murderer, okay, she would just kick her heels together and fly up out of reach. Why not? If she had already started glowing, well, anything could happen now.

Angelica

But there was an angel coughing there, sitting down casually on the altar.

'I've got a bit of a hack,' she explained, 'my homeopath said phosphorus would work, but it hasn't helped me out yet.'

Yes. It was a 'she'. Despite the fact that the nun had always been taught that angels were sexless, gender-free. She didn't remember who had told her that, however. It wasn't like angels were mentioned by name all that often in the Bible, anyhow, only twice, Gabriel and Michael, and two and a half times, she reckoned, if you were allowed to count Lucifer.

'Then again, I really haven't been taking the phosphorus at regular intervals,' the angel admitted to the nun.

Like the nun before her, the angel also got to her feet and stretched. Her frame was sleek and androgynous, but it was irrefutably female. She had high small breasts and since she stood immodestly, with feet apart while she stretched and yawned, you could even see a bit of luminescent labia peeping out from between her thighs. Also, the angel had pubic hair. And when this heavenly messenger – who in general radiated white – spread her arms out, her wings shook, and the nun saw that each feather was a different shade and each glowed as if lit from a lamp underneath: apricot, rose, bright blue, darkest black that still shone, blood-red, green, peach, orange, yellow, violet and, of course, all the metallics like silver and bronze and gold, that goes without saying.

The nun remembered reading that white was all colours together, so maybe this whiteness was more concentrated in the angel's flesh, as it were, and more diffused in the feathered wings where the white light burst out into rainbows. The nun had that warm tight feeling again, looking at the angel.

'If you want to kiss me, feel free,' said the angel, 'I'm sure you'd enjoy it.'

The nun was only a trifle embarrassed that the angel could read minds. At the same time it was quite exhilarating, because it was being made quite clear that such desires were nothing at all to be ashamed of.

Five fireflies landed on the nun's arm in a line, blending into her own naked glow in the shiny green glen, and they travelled along for the ride when she joined the angel atop the altar and put her fingers up, uncertainly, to stroke the angel's feathers.

The angel's whole body rippled with pleasure. 'Do that again,' she told the nun. The nun caressed a soft avocado-coloured feather then, and watched the angel's face crease into ecstasy as she did so. It was quite extraordinary and it filled the nun with a kind of pride.

'My name is Margaret,' said the nun, shyly. 'What's yours?'

'It's Angelica, of course.' The angel seemed a bit snippy that the nun hadn't guessed. 'Nothing daft like Angela. I hate that name.'

'Oh, I completely agree,' said the nun happily, 'I've always disliked the name Angela. But Angelica is a lovely, lovely name. *Quite* different,' she added, stroking the angel's other wing with a bit more confidence and enjoying the rapture that passed over the angel's features as she did so.

The nun now realised that there were flowers dotted in between the trees around the glen, *herba angelica*, an aromatic umbelliferous plant. It seemed exactly right, in the circumstances. If she were ever to bake a cake for the angel, it suddenly occurred to her, she would decorate the frosting with candied stalks of angelica, as well.

The angel smiled at her, tenderly, and wrapped her long arms round the nun, pulling them close together. There was a tingling feeling where their crotches met, and their breasts matched the nipples of the other quite perfectly, and the nun felt that warmth now from her feet to her groin to her areolas to the back of her neck and then out to her fingers clasped round the angel's trim waist. And then the angel folded her wings round the nun, and pressed her closer as they stood there on the altar, and put her lips to the nun's lips.

Angelica

The kiss was wonderful. It felt just perfect. It made the nun think of Jesus and love and all that was right with the world. The angel's tongue in her mouth had the purity of desire, and the nun began to tremble, clasped there in those huge wings and by the angel's arms around her waist, and then she began to kiss back as well. She shifted her own hands so she could run them up and down the angel's body, which was a delight beyond compare. The angel's glowing skin was smooth like a living flower petal, and just the feel of the angel made the nun go wet between her legs.

Which turned out to be a good thing, because the angel was releasing her and urging her down, down, to lie with her on the overgrown grass of the top stone step, and the angel was kissing the nun between her legs, and the nun felt such stabs of clear need that she shifted position so that her face too was at the angel's thighs. And when the nun licked at her there, the angel was certainly not sexless; she was the best things of sex that have ever been named, and her nectar there tasted like water, but such sweet water, and the nun wondered whether the wetness would leave glowing traces all over her face.

But also, the nun was enjoying the angel's persistent licking on her own sex, a steady rhythm that changed for the nun from shivers of pleasure that concentrated themselves at the nun's hole and little bud and then grew to the whole area below her waist. Between her legs she was soaked with the sap of desire, and then the beat of pleasure overtook her just as the glow had worked itself from her finger along the rest of her flesh, and she bucked and tried to move her sex more rapidly against the regular licking of the angel's heavenly tongue. She could feel just the slightest tickle of the angel's wings on her back, and this made her even more desirous. And all the while she ran the flat of her own tongue back from hole to bud across the angel's sex, which had turned from white to glowing red with need, and the rapture grew greater and greater. The nun jerked her hips forward again and again towards the point of the angel's tongue, trying to prolong the final ripples of pleasure, bitter yet candied, that made her itch for one more wave, one more crest of tingly bliss.

When her head came out of the clouds, though she was as wet as anything and the angel's tongue was still spinning pleasure on her sex in the aftermath, she kept up her own part of the bargain, as it were. She licked the angel into an orgasm on the stone step, so that the angel at last went all purple, then blue, then ebony, then fuschia with pleasure and cried out silver tears and laughed and sang out the most beautiful rendition of Violetta's *Follie!* aria the nun had ever heard.

Above them, the trees glowed with appreciation.

The angel rose to her feet and, though she was still shaky herself, she chivalrously helped the nun up as well, and wrapped arms and wings around her as she had before, and kissed her for a long, long time.

'Forget Celia,' the angel told the nun, 'forget Mother Wilgefortis. Forget them all. You know yourself what feels right.'

'Okay.' The nun's response was so speedy that she grinned, at herself.

The angel kissed her on the nose and the nun barely had time to wonder whether she'd get freckles there before the angel stretched out one hand, and the nun grasped it hard, for she had a thing about heights, and they both rose above the discredited shrine, like Superman and Lois Lane, the nun thought, that's really great, and a chain of intrepid fireflies followed them up into the clouds as well, for light after all attracts light.

Nugget Nancy, Queen of the Yukon

Nugget Nancy, Queen of the Yukon

My mother had extracted my promise that I should not wander without my brother's escort on those decks which most lured my attention, but as soon as Mother retired to sleep, so did Alex retire to the gambling tables, and I was left to my own devices.

My heart was beating quickly and my cheeks began to turn red as soon as I passed through the curtains, vermilion and velvet and threadbare (in places) all at once, that separated the lower deck from the upper, and this act ushered in a feeling of excitement so urgent that my very limbs began to tremble, and my palms went damp.

There was every variety of person in the room: roughened men with unkempt beards and red swollen faces; women of both light and dark complexions who wore paint and looked as gaudy as actresses; serious and rather handsome young men with black flashing eyes. And there was so much tobacco smoke that a vapour seemed to float above the room's inhabitants, and I observed more than one of the ladies – if I might call them that – withdraw a cigar from between her lips in order to exhale. And the man at the piano – a dapper fellow in a fine suit and hat – was smoking too, pausing to tap off ashes as he tinkled out a melody to which many did sing along, although few matched the pianist's skill and the chorus reminded me somewhat of the caterwauling that takes

Astrid Fox

place back home in Illinois on summer nights. I do not know if they will have cats in Alaska. I suppose they will.

All this I stared at in wonder, scarcely daring to breathe, and the *Katrina Simone* did rock so that room before me swayed, and I struggled to keep my footing.

'Lily! You must leave this deck immediately!' It was my brother Alex striding towards me, eyes bright from whiskey and fair hair tousled in an untidy fashion. He took my arm and led me away with only a bit of a struggle, though I kept looking back over my shoulder at the smoking room and at a flash of green fabric that had caught my eye, but he tugged at me so and pulled me between the old curtains so quickly that whatever had piqued my vision was not made clear.

We stood just on the other side of the curtains, both breathing at a ragged pace from the tussle, and I fancied that I could still feel the curtains – once soft, now toughened, velvet – over my face and throat for, as we had pushed through like Moses through his sea, I fancied that I could still smell the scent of stale cigarillos and something else that clung to the fabric of the curtains – possibly an inexpensive perfume. It was a memory speedily coined, only at best mere seconds old, and yet to me it now seemed the most wondrous and exciting memory of my life.

'What the devil were you doing in there?' Alex reprimanded in far harsher a tone than his normal manner. 'I'm going to have to tell Mother now, and you'll have the tongue-lashing of your life.'

'She would be equally perturbed upon hearing that you made a dash for the card tables,' I parried, 'and left me bored and idle in the upper galley with nothing but a pack of elderly matrons and their lecherous husbands to amuse me.'

Alex first looked shocked that I would be aware of, much less mention, carnal desires, and then glared at me, biting his lip and saying nothing for a moment. Eventually he seemed to come to some interior conclusion and then, thus resolved, took my arm

Nugget Nancy, Queen of the Yukon

and led me towards the upper deck.

'We won't tell anyone. And you won't go back to those quarters.'

I nodded, and kept my own peace. (And my own counsel.)

For I wanted, very much, to go back to the room.

The next day, Alex shot me a terrible look when once again Mother left us behind in the upper gallery, for she was tired and claimed a rest in the cabin alone. He took cards from his pocket and laid out a spread of Patience. But the name was not apt, for first he began to sigh and then I watched him cheat two times. When even then he did not win, he bundled up the deck again in his handkerchief, and he was fair twitching. It was then that I realised that my dear brother was afflicted with the gambling fever, just a bit, and the reason why he shifted so was because he was anxious to make his way toward the *real* card tables, and yet there was his duty as my chaperone in Mother's absence, as well.

He agonised several minutes more, walking the length of the galley and peering out at the choppy waves, before at last he said, 'Hang it!' under his breath and pushed past me, though not before adding, 'YOU STAY HERE!' in a forceful tone, as if the words were block capitals written out on a playbill's list of *dramatis personae*.

Do you think I stayed? It must be clear, already, that mine is not a mind easily commanded and is also a mind easily made curious. I waited six minutes and then I, too, left the upper decks. Old Mrs Enstelson had a supercilious tilt to her features as I passed by and she lifted her skirts and drew in her breath in a hiss. I imagine her irritation was born of her husband's ill-disguised eagerness to engage me in conversation, as well as breathe over my décolleté.

I passed through the curtains with the same sense of anticipation as I had felt the day before. A woman snickered at me, and I could guess that she supposed me callow. But I did not concentrate on her snickers for long, nor on the raucous singing that greeted my ears again, nor on the riotous colours of sky-blue, violet, wine-red that glared the whole room round, for there was only one colour I saw, and that was the colour of the dress of the woman playing at the piano. Nor was her green costume, dipped low at the neck and raised high on the calves, exposing a daring few inches above the ankle, the most vibrant thing about her, for her hair was red as that hero of Mr Twain's, and I suspect it was tinted. I thought she was quite beautiful. Her fingers moved nimbly across the keys and she segued from 'Swanee River' to 'The Bowery' as quick as that, and the crowds drew round her as the mournful melody became a boisterous, swinging sing-along, and the whole roomed shouted in chorus, *'I had one of the DEVIL's own nights, I'll never go there anymore! The Bowery –! The Bowery –!'* and then I saw that the pianistress was looking at me alone, and mouthing the words with her painted lips, and with a bit of a devil's glint in her own eye, it has to be said. And I stood there frozen, because the rest of the smoking and carousing crowd might have been singing loud and looking at the woman in the green dress, but the woman in the green dress was looking only at me.

She finished the song with a bang, to much hand-clapping, and then brayed in a loud voice, 'Well, this little's ditty's made me a trifle thirsty now. Who will buy the girl a drink?'

There was much competition and jostling and whistling amongst men eager to do exactly this, and one even took his poke from his pocket and emptied a little gold nugget into his palm and shouted that it was a small price to pay for the privilege of buying a drink for Nugget Nancy, Queen of the Yukon. And it was at that point, when he and another bristly miner began to chest off in what looked to develop to fisticuffs, that I found my voice at last.

'I will buy you a drink, Miss.' My voice rang out clear as a bell and the entire room turned to gape at me, even the miners intent on mutual bodily harm.

'Well, well, well.' She rose from the piano and glided towards me like a cat on a bird, and I began to quake a little, for I did not know what it was that made me speak out so, other than the fact that she had moved something in me as she sat there and played both a melancholy song and a vulgar one; the way she had let her fingers skim between sadness and fun.

'And you're a fine little duchess, ain't you?' said the woman the miner had called Nugget Nancy as she now stood in front of me. 'Do you think perhaps you've found yourself on quite the wrong deck, hmm? And what will you use to pay for my drink – perhaps your mother's locket, or a gilded token from your sweetheart?'

I flushed, but I put my hand into my pocket and took out the little purse where I keep coins and I opened it to show her that I did have some funding for a drink, though of course I did not know how much one would cost.

'Show us your other snatch!' shouted a man off to the left in a roaring voice, but Nancy turned around with a glare and then her eyes darted back to the purse that I held out to her tight in my trembling fingers.

She let out a great whinny of a laugh then, and clapped her hands together. 'A drink with a duchess! I ain't going to say no to that, boys, now am I? Not compared to trash like yourselves!'

There were loud protests of 'Oh, Nan!' and half-hearted pleadings of suit, but by that point she had taken my arm and was leading me off to the side of the room.

'I'm not a duchess, you know.' I was confused; I thought maybe she actually thought I was and I didn't want to embarrass her.

'No, you ain't, darlin'. But you have saved me from wasting ten minutes with this ragamuffin troupe, and for that I'd call you my queen. Now! Here we are!'

We stood now by the bar-counter and two gruff men, dirty as orphans, rose up to make room for us and so we acquired two seats. Once rested, Nancy called out for a gin and I asked for another, and I paid for them both, though my fingers shook as I did so. The populace of the room darted us glances from time to time, but soon another pianist took his place on the stool, and the room shook with the melody of 'A Hot Time in the Old Town Tonight' and again I saw how Nugget Nancy turned her attention towards me.

She was not old, not too much older than myself, anyway; I guessed her to be two-and-twenty or at oldest four-and-twenty. Her figure in her corset was as curved as the figure 8 that boys skate into ponds; her red hair shone like a lantern; her green eyes were huge, and fringed with gold-dark lashes, and her mouth just a perfect tiny rosebud, and I could well understand why these rough men fought for the chance of a few minutes alone with her. I sensed she was curious why I was there, and she confirmed this by asking why a nice girl like myself troubled herself to talk to a woman like *herself*.

I did not understand her direct meaning, though in truth I had my suspicions, but I said that I admired her songs and wondered at fingers that could convey both sadness and spirit and wasn't that the sign of a sensitive soul, after all?

At this she laughed loudly again and got straight up in my face so that I could smell the gin on her breath and see the glitter of her eye, and she said, 'Well, I'll be damned. I've heard of some sneaky missionaries in my time, but I've never yet heard of them drinking with you first, or using slips of girls to sermonise, neither!'

The gin was flaming my throat as I protested, saying that I had come down to the lower deck on my own accord and not on account of any missionary zeal, at which point she seemed to calm down a little, and her eyes turned from suspicion to frank perplexion.

'You came down here on your own?'

'I did,' I confirmed.

'What a bright gem you are.' Her smile was softer this time, nearly gentle, and her eyes looked wet for a moment. 'Well now, my sweetheart, I do thank you for your kind drink and now you've had a taste of excitement down here, but I think it's high time a pretty girl like yourself took your leave, for there's some here that might take advantage of a soft unschooled kitten.'

'I can stand my own stead, thank you very much,' I retorted rather snippily, and took another big gulp of stinging gin, at which she merely laughed and took the glass away from me and half-pushed me off my chair towards the red curtains as one might do to a favourite but irritating dog.

'Get on, you. And I don't want to see you in here again.' But her voice was not as brash as it had been before, and she gave me a wink as I stood there forlornly, though she didn't look at me as she shimmied towards the piano in that shiny green satin dress and her fingers picked out the tune of 'She is More to Be Pitied Than Censured' and this time her voice was as sweet as a nightingale's, and when she raised her head once during the mournful song and saw me standing by the red curtains, still staring at her as she sang the words, *'She is only a lassie who ventured, on Life's stormy path ill-advised'*, she gave me another big wink and nodded towards the curtains. I do not think anyone else noticed, for they were all struck into thoughtful silence by the sweetness of the tune and even some of the more gruff men were coughing and dabbing at their eyes with smutty handkerchiefs. By then I was standing on the other side of the curtains and feeling my heart pound, and I could hear her voice pierce all the way through the red fabric, sweet as a needle through satin and twice as keen.

Do not scorn her with words fierce and bitter,
Do not laugh at her shame and downfall,
For a moment just stop and consider,
That a man was the cause of it all.

I stumbled when I entered our stateroom, and my mother looked up at me with an alarmed expression on her face. 'Lily,' she said, 'are you drunk?'

The next day the ocean pounded our boat and we were all sick, but the day after that was calm in comparison and while Mother and Alex played Whist in the upper deckroom, I complained of a stomach pain. Mother had been concerned about the extent of my ill health the day before – though I had heard it said that gin affects the constitution in uncomfortable ways – and urged me to retire back to bed, which was just as I had wished.

I had taken particular pains with my appearance that morning and as such my bangs were arranged and my dress was my favourite, a pale-yellow one of silk, and I had put powder on my face. I had a difficult time looking ill enough to convince Mother that I was ailing, for my cheeks were flushed; I could feel them when I took my gloves off and held my palms to my visage. When I felt my fingers there, I remembered to be mightily grateful that Mother had chosen this water route up to St Michael as opposed to the Chilkoot Pass, where Alexander had told me people's fingers frequently froze and were then snapped off like sticks and by the time any company cleared the Chilkoot, those left alive would have just paws and no fingers left at all. As far as my assumed illness, the powder helped, and soon I was pushing my way through the curtains as I had before.

This time the room recognised me, for the men hooted out, 'Here's the lady again!' and this shamed me, but I didn't think long on it because there she was, in the green dress, the woman they called Nugget Nancy, and she started to laugh and said, 'Duchess, I told you to stick to your own decks.'

'I'd like another gin,' I said boldly to the bartender.

And Nugget Nancy drew near me to sigh and say, 'Duchess, this is no place for a lady, whether you got yourself a taste for

Nugget Nancy, Queen of the Yukon

gin or not.'

'You are not a lady.' The words escaped my mouth and I wished I had bitten them back, but I have always had a problem with my hasty tongue. For a moment, I fancied she might cut me by turning round, sniffing and raising her nose as the ladies on the upper deck did to women such as her.

But instead she laughed again, a short sharp laugh, and she said, 'That is true, I am not.' She stood close to me and whispered in my ear, and her red curls rustled against my neck. 'But hear this, little duchess, I am soon to be richer than any lady on this boat, well-born or not, and richer than any man too.'

'We are here to make our fortune as well,' I told her.

She looked confused.

'My mother, my brother and I,' I clarified. 'My father is dead, but my mother is a dressmaker, and she has heard it said that she can earn five hundred dollars a month, and my brother will find himself a claim, and we shall make our fortune.'

Nancy looked concerned. 'I fear your mother has heard wrong. It is not nearly that much. And as for your brother finding a claim, well, they are all well taken by now, and most of them sluiced clean of both nuggets and dust as well.'

At that point someone screamed, 'Play, Nancy, sing!' and so she left me for the piano and some of the bright girls rose to the tables and stepped up on them, and raised their skirts far above the knee, and higher still, and then I did not dare to keep looking, and then the girls danced to the tune that Nancy was pounding out – I could hear it from the clip-clop of their heels – and I looked straight at Nancy there in her green dress and her voice was throaty and exciting too; it filled me with envy and wanderlust, the same itch that I felt when Mother first told us that we were heading for the Yukon, and Nugget Nancy winked her usual wink at me.

The men of the sporting girls went round with their hats and other men threw coins into them. When the bright girls' men reached me and held out the hat, I fled.

That night I could not sleep. I had Nancy's face before me in the dark, and she seemed the bravest person I had ever met, man or woman, and I wondered how she would make her fortune. Perhaps she had a poke, hidden away, or a claim already. What courage and fire! Her hair itself seemed to crackle with her determination. And she was beautiful! And she sang like a bird, and sometimes like a sailor, and all the songs were equally thrilling!

I tossed and turned until my mother reminded me that in two days we would be in St Michael, and it was best to be rested upon our arrival. My mother's voice was weary, for in my excitement I had kept her awake as well. Alex, though, snored on the other side of the stateroom. When first we had embarked, my mother had questioned the propriety of a son boarding in the same quarters as his mother and sister, but when she learned that others had been forced to share accommodation with actresses, she did not complain further.

I tried to keep still then, but I grew to wonder what it would be like to share quarters with an actress or perhaps even a scandalous singer like Nugget Nancy, and I grew so feverish with the adventure of this idea that I lay in the dark with my eyes wide open, considering, although for my mother's sake in the berth beneath me I did not squirm. But think if it were just Nancy and I in the one room! I would ask her how long it took for her to memorise the words to her songs, and I would watch as she stood before the mirror and patted down her green dress and perhaps even as she powdered her lower neck, if it was her custom to do an act so risqué.

That night, when finally I did sleep, I had the most peculiar dreams.

'You do not look well, Lily,' said my mother when morning came,

'I fear you will need to stay in this cabin all day, for you must be healthy and have your wits about you when we disembark in St Michael tomorrow, for I do not know truly all that will await us there.'

It was the first time I heard my mother voice care over the purpose of our journey, and this made me shudder a little, but mainly I protested that I was fine and wanted to get up (I did not tell her, nor Alex, that I intended to go back to the scandalous room yet again), but Mother insisted and so I lay surly and irritable while Alex and Mother took their breakfast above, returned briefly, and then later in the morning left once again to play at Whist on the upper deck. There was a great stomping overhead at one point, and this annoyed me because although I was not truly ill I *was* genuinely tired, and the sound was vexing.

Soon Alex rushed in, cheeks aglow, to tell me that the whole boat was running, and when I asked him what that meant he told me that each man would link his hands to the shoulders of the man in front of them and they would begin to run, and then more linked on, respectable ladies and actresses alike, and then the whole line would run about the deck and everyone was laughing while the whole group whirled in a great circle, holding on tight to the one in front, and the entire ship was laughing together, and even Mother had been drawn into the fun, although now she was breathlessly recovering.

Alex's tale only made me simmer, wishing that I had had part of that fun, and then I also wondered whether Nugget Nancy had been amongst the running, and whether Alex had stood behind her. The idea of my brother touching her shoulders, laying his fingers on her fine shiny green dress, made me even more cross, though I could not fathom why.

Eventually Alex quit the cabin and in his absence I dressed carefully and quickly, pulling at my stays and stepping into my dark blue dress with the lace at the décolleté, and when I left the stateroom I looked left and right, but there was no one there in the hall, and I hurried as quickly as I could to the piano room on the lower deck.

She was there, sitting alone at the piano bench, and I saw her before she saw me, so I had a chance to look at her for a moment. That was when I realised how truly comely she was – she might be brass, but she was also a beauty, as much as any portrait I'd ever seen.

'Duchess.' She looked up and I saw that I had frightened her, which seemed an odd thing, a girl like me frightening a woman like her. 'Why are you not running with the others?' she asked, and her smile was disarmingly gentle.

'I couldn't sleep last night,' I told her, feeling more bold than I ever had before in my life, 'I was thinking of you.'

She looked at me and she smiled again and then she gave out a little sigh. 'You're not the first in skirts to say that to me,' she said, 'but understand this, Duchess, I ain't been wooed by a man yet and there's not a lady that can tumble me yet, neither.' She saw me blanch a little and step back, and she let out a cackle and it was not nice this time at all. 'Oh! Crude words shock you, do they, Duchess?'

'My name is Lily.'

'Your fine little ears haven't heard much of that language, I reckon. Well, you wait until tomorrow in St Michael, and then you'll hear some talk that will sting your ears. This is my third trip up, and third time's the charm, but the first time I was younger than you, and the only purse I had was the one between my legs – Oh Duchess! You're shocked! Yes, between my sweet thighs, and when I say I've not been tumbled yet by man or woman I mean beaten, flat on my back, defeated. I'm going up to this frozen hell for one last try and I aim to make my fortune this time and I ain't going to let a snooty-nosed little lady like yourself make me feel guilty one bit.'

Nugget Nancy, Queen of the Yukon

It was true that I was trembling a trace, and perhaps even true that I was crying a bit at her words, for they did shock me, I couldn't deny it, but I was also transfixed, for as she spoke she did so with such passion that, despite her bitterness, I remembered the mournful quality to her voice when she sang the sad song, and the exciting quality when she sang the sprightly one, and the bawdy quality when she sang the scandalous one, and I envied her and admired her more right then than I had ever loved anyone before on earth, including the sainted memory of my own dear father.

I stepped closer, and she seemed confused that I had not been stung so much by her words that I had run away, but she was no bee, or if she were then I wanted to be a flower. I wanted her to be drawn to me as I was to her. I wanted her lips on mine, my hands on her shoulders like they might have been if we had run the boat together and had had the luck to be placed one after another in the running line. I kissed her then, and she froze like one of those men Alex had told me about on Chilkoot Pass, frozen solid through and dead as a spoon, and then I put my hand to her chignon. I just wanted to see the hair escape from its knots, the red strands shine in my fingers for a moment – my heart was knocking, I could scarcely breathe – just as I had imagined it would fall if we shared quarters and I were to watch her unmake her *toilette*.

She looked at me with her heavy-lidded eyes, and the bitterness left them, and she pulled me down into her arms and pressed her paint-stained lips to my own. She clasped her hands round my neck and held me there close to her, and it is fair to say that I did not exactly trouble myself to struggle loose. All around me I could hear a great thudding. At first I did think it was my heart, for I admit to a weakness for romantic novels, but of course it was merely the drumming of feet overhead, for folks were at the 'running' again, but I cared not because my hands were on Nancy's creamy shoulders, and her teeth were on my own throat, biting, nipping, and though it stung it was not unpleasurable, and though her breath smelled faint of whiskey I did not dislike it, because her mouth was wet on mine.

And I opened my eyes to see hers closed, and the boat shook from a strong wave, and we fell closer into each other. And then my hands were stroking her form, just as hers were stroking mine. She was moaning, and then humming, and I thought she was going to burst into one of her songs, but she gave a soft groan instead, and pulled me closer, and her hands traced my bosom, over the cotton, over the stays, which made me blush.

'Duchess!' she half-shouted, laughing, 'you're a jade, you are!'

I was fair embarrassed at her words, but at the same time they stimulated and thrilled me and, as my hand was now caressing her ankle since she had kicked off her shoes in her merriment, I pushed the same hand further up her calf, feeling the ribs of her stockings, and indeed it made my own cheeks glow to hear how she giggled as I did so. I pushed my hand up a little further and Nugget Nancy grew very quiet then and did not laugh at all. I had half a mind to quote Shakespeare's Mistress Quickly, but feared she would think me daft for a such a reference. I supposed such thoughts came from sheer trepidation on my part anyway, for my fingers shook as my hand stroked further up until it met the flesh of her thigh – oh, it was so soft, softer than even her cheek or her smooth shoulders, and in place of her mirth she was now breathing very fast little breaths. My hand went quickly then; I do not know how it lost its initial cautiousness and subtlety, for all at once my fingers were plunged into the wetness between her legs, and I was thrusting then into her with the simple fierceness of my dreams the night before, and my fingers were tight within her hole, and I could *smell* her hole, even through the whiskey on her breath, even through the cheap perfume, I could smell the scent of her, and it smelled like me.

Nancy's fists grasped the piano seat, and my hand was working on her rapidly, my curls loose, my neck and bosom perspiring as I hoped that what often felt good for me would in a like manner affect the same sweetness for her. And so my fingers twisted and curled and prodded into the slick jammy hole of hers and I could feel the same pooling between my own thighs; I would be as slippery as she, if ever Nugget Nancy were to touch me there as I now touched her, which I hoped mightily she would have occasion some time to do, and the boat shook with the sea swells, and the feet stomped overhead, and as I bent down on it the piano tinkled out an unfamilar tune in an arrangement that I am sure even the songstress Nugget Nancy Queen of the Yukon had never heard before.

We went back to her stateroom and lay in her bed the rest of the afternoon, and none of her sporting-girl friends seemed to note or care much as we kissed each other throughout the day.

Nancy told me tales of men who teased the ladies by dropping nuggets cold as ice down the front of their dresses, and how the victims were always both furious and gratified, and how girls sometimes took up with the Indian men, for they were treated far better by some of them, and bore them babies, and spoke their tongue, and of how the snow froze up even your tears into little knives on your cheeks, which would then fall down and snip off your toes, so it was better not to cry in the Yukon at all, and she told me of girls who had fallen for men with sleek mustaches and fine ways only to find that they had hard fists and forced the girls to work for gold that paid for the men's expensive mustache waxes, and of girls who had sold themselves for only a night for the price of a nugget as big as my own right hand, the one from which Nancy had so recently taken such pleasure, and also of girls who'd been wellborn as I, who now had fallen and despaired of their lots, and shot themselves as well as their beaux.

And also, and Nancy was quite firm about this last story, about how a lass could hit pay dirt, had she wits and tolerance of gruff behaviour, and something finer to look forward to in her bed at night.

When I heard Alex calling my name down the corridor for the fourth time, I stole away from her red curls and soft bosom and satiny thighs at last, for I did not want my mother to think I had drowned.

'You've been drinking,' Alex said. 'I've already told Mother you had been in the gaming room. She has chosen not to believe me.'

'You've been drinking as well; I can smell it on your lips,' I retorted, 'And as for me and how I choose to spend my leisure time, what of it?'

My brother turned on his heel and I made sure to rinse my mouth before climbing into the bunk over Mother's head, Mother who was so furious she could barely bring herself to wish me good dreams.

She remained pale and tight-lipped as the boat bumped its way onto the dock at St Michael the next morning. I stood with Mother and Alex and our luggage and wondered whether Mother would find our fortune here, or if Alex truly would stake a fruitful claim once he made it to the poking fields.

The actresses and the rough men and the sporting girls stood ahead of us, and I could just make out one of the figures in a parrot-green dress, with brassy strawberry curls piled high, and I thought of how some sporting girls wore belts of gold as pay for their troubles, as Nancy had told me, and I wondered whether there was such a shine under that fine green dress.

At that point the huge crowd of men on the shore, for there were few women, gave a great roar and began to chant, and I realised that this was because they had recognised the bright feathers of my nightingale. My mother turned up her nose and Alex sniffed, but I merely felt pride deep inside me, burning like

Nugget Nancy, Queen of the Yukon

a sudden fever down below my waist, like a hidden golden belt. Then the nightingale turned, and I realised that she was not watching the men, but watching me, and then she stretched out a hand, and then I looked at Mother and Alex.

'It's all right, Mother,' I shouted as I stepped away, 'for I intend to make a fortune, too!' My mother nodded, but she looked worried and uneasy, and I thought that perhaps she did not understand what I was saying.

I began to run down into the crowd that was pushing along the gangplank, to stake my claim, and Nancy grabbed me by the hand and pulled me to her and kissed me, and even all the rough folk grinned to see such sisterly affection, for the Yukon is cold and often friendless, so it is said. And Nancy kissed me again, and I knew that whether I struck it rich or lost it all, when I thought of her I would shine, and shine, and shine.

For we might be in the North where limbs and fingers and toes turned first white then black from frost and then fell off, but all the same she was an alchemist, a Midas; for when her fingers touched me, I turned to purest Klondike gold – yes, the warm, living fingers of the red-haired, green-eyed songstress of the North, Nugget Nancy, truly Queen of the Yukon!

Allure

Allure

Under the semitropical sea, the water was a lovely shade of blue, and bright-red anemones wiggled their fronds in the wake of yellow-and-green fish with impressive dorsal fins. Here and there, a crab scuttled across the sand at the ocean floor. Soon more and more purple fish passed by, along with a cumulus cloud of several pale-pink jellyfish.

This may all sound like a Windows for Word screensaver, but trust me: it really was that colourful down below.

Just around the corner from a medium-sized shipwreck, perched on top of an accommodating mass of rose-coloured coral, two mermaids kissed passionately, their hair flowing out behind them with the current – gold-green (swimmer's hair) and pitch-black tresses, respectively. Their kiss was almost violently intense, belying the relatively chilled-out tropical depths because Sandy, for that was the name of the dark-haired demi-lass, and Coral, that was the blonde, had a groovy kind of love.

Their mouths, one plum and the other bright-red, met and parted. Coral lifted up Sandy's beautiful dark hair and kissed the back of her neck with that bright little pout. The other mermaid's breasts were two tan cones in the water, ones with strawberry-red tips, not that either of them had ever tasted a strawberry. Coral pinched at Sandy's strawberry nipples with love, with force, until the peaks went stone-hard in the chill water, until the other siren wrapped arms and tail round Coral and pulled her into yet another fierce kiss that eventually turned dreamy.

From up above the shipwreck, the sun shone hard down on the water, and the rays that reached the two mermaids down below shivered inconstantly across their bare breasts and drifting hair and long arms and scaly, silver-mud-green tails.

Inevitably Sandy and Coral admitted that they'd have to go to work – they could hardly bunk off and pull a sickie for the third time that week – and they smiled secret smiles at each other and then reluctantly took out shell combs and began to work through the tangles of each other's streaming hair, in preparation.

A young woman of twenty-eight walked along the shoreline. She tried to think of nothing, picking up attractive rocks from time to time. The wind was quite bad today. She stopped for a moment and attempted to braid up her waist-length hair so that it wouldn't whip up around her face, but she had stupidly forgotten rubber bands, and the wind loosened her braid soon enough.

It was nice here on the Belize beach; she was glad she'd left him back at the hotel taverna. How awful to break up on holiday. It wasn't that they both hadn't seen it coming; it was just that she didn't understand why it had to happen here, now, two days left of the charter break, and they'd both have to pussyfoot around each other until they took the hydrofoil back to Belize City and boarded the plane back to Stansted Airport. Then home sweet home to good old Chelmsford, and it would probably all get a lot easier after that.

The tide washed a shell up on the wet sand. She picked it up. It was one of those empty charmers that always made her think of spiral staircases, a Cornetto of a shell. It was big considering it was of the twisty sort, just a little smaller than her pinkie. She wondered what it would be like to have a shell as a finger prosthetic. It would be beautiful but people would stare. She put it up to her ear. It was constructed wrong. She couldn't hear anything. Besides, the roar of the wind in the outside world was quite loud enough as it was.

It was lucky it was so hot. That was one of the things they'd bickered about that finally pushed them over the edge. He'd liked the cool shade of the tavernas and she'd preferred walking along the beaches, just as she was walking now. Her mood brightened: she was doing exactly what she wanted to be doing for once. Lovely. The sand squished in between her bare toes. She unbuttoned her shirt and removed it, tying it round her waist, and she stuffed her bra in her trouser pocket. Even better. She didn't even care that she had no lotion on and would burn. One of the downsides to freedom, so be it.

There was a stirring near the edge of the tide. The water was transparently clear. She saw two mermaids on their backs floating beneath the water, like they were basking in the shallows just as she had basked on her towel on the sand earlier that morning. They were holding hands and blowing bubbles up on purpose to the top of the waves, to get her attention. But even in the short time since the beach girl had first stopped and stared, the tide had already gone out enough to reveal just the mermaids' mouths above the water, rosy-lipped and open, parted. The dark-haired mermaid's lips were lushly purple, very full, and the blonde must have been wearing Lorelei by Loréal to get a shade of scarlet so bright.

She looked at the two mouths there, just an inch above the bob of the blue-green water, and she lowered herself until she put the tips of her breasts in the water, and she let them suck on them, and it was the most erotic thing she'd ever felt. The water lapped against her stomach and her throat. She held herself there, trembling above their mouths. From a distance her position looked like a swimmer on the stand before a race, poised, nearly ready to dive in and let herself go.

Sweet Poison

Sweet Poison

She was walking near the woods looking for edible vegetation and berries; the snow was still melting on the ground and occasionally ripe flashes of cranberries and pink-orange salmonberries peeked out from the dwindling clusters of snow. Her basket was far from full, but she still hesitated before entering the woods. The hush in the trees was whispering quiet as she picked her way through the bracken and the melting ice, searching for tell-tale bits of ferns she could dig for their coiled roots. She went on in this manner through the late afternoon woods, the sunlight hot against her neck; her feet were aching and wet from the cold. In some places the snow had melted entirely, leaving a damp flat tundra of grass tendrils and ripening moss. She thought she saw a clearing up ahead, so took a breath and continued deeper in the woods.

She did not expect to see what she found in the clearing: a dead young man lying on a bed of unseasonably green leaves. She walked closer, in her wonder forgetting her cold stinging feet and the gnawing in her stomach. The taut skin of his entire body was white but his hair shone red. His hair was the crimson of blood and currants. Past the pout of his lips and all the way to his waist flowed his hair. She wanted to touch his hair, eat it, swallow it down, rub herself in it. A beautiful man. As if still tensed with life, his cheeks were dimpled. His long eyelashes were strawberry-blond shadows against them; he looked as if he might raise his lids at any second. The early spring sunlight through the trees dappled the young man's face. A beautiful man. But he didn't breathe.

She drew still closer. She knew he was dead, but there was – yes, the wet of tears left upon his face; sweet poison was raining down from his eyes. It was poison that had killed him. She knew the signs and she could see them in his stiff limbs. On the green bed and near his lips, she noticed the broken shrub of mistletoe by his hand, with its characteristic white berries. That had to have been it; that had to have been the poison. He lay prone – his face stilled into a smile despite his tears, the masses of his hair blowing in the forest breeze. The leaves were unspoilt green scallops around his bright body – like him, they looked to be hanging on to life's edges. It was poison that had killed him, and it felt like poison that ran trembling through her veins as she looked at his entire naked body.

And the whole of his body was perfect – his limbs, his cock, his neck and torso were all perfectly carved. A beautiful man. She dropped her basket and her spade. She bent her head down to kiss his cold lips, and she didn't feel the cold; she felt warmth, a warm current running through her, her cunt tightening. When she raised her head, she admired his nipples and their exquisite tiny beauty on his bare chest. She bent her head down to gently suckle at one nipple and this time it was cold, ice-cold but soft against her tongue. She felt the brush of his hair against her neck. She drew back. She was as alone in the forest as she had been before, the birds still twittering the trees. The sun beat down on the undergrowth, but there was no one but her and the young man there.

But she knew something had changed in the woods. There was a crackling around her but no source. She found herself breathing quickly; she listened to the trees, her senses heightened. There was a poison inside her. But by then the crackling had stopped and she heard nothing. She knew she ought to be heading back and her feet were beginning to ache again; she grew dizzy and light-headed. She looked down at the young man and again she felt the pulse inside her: she bent her head once more to his nipple and lightly sucked it. It turned hard in her mouth and she bit lightly at it before the implications of its rigidity hit her. She let her mouth release it and, though her heart quickened, without obvious haste she raised herself to face what was there. One of her hands remained on his bare smooth chest, and she felt the skin grow warm beneath her hand.

The young man had raised his lids. His eyes were green as the leaves on which he lay, and she was aware that he was observing her. Have I brought him back from the dead? she wondered. But then the man reached for her; she closed her eyes and she felt him stick his tongue in her mouth. All of it, all that could fit deep in her mouth.

The lust that she felt was so heavy that her body reacted before her mind. Her mouth was sucking in his thickened tongue and pushing her own tongue under his before she was aware of it; her body had thrust her sex against his; her hands had taken his and pushed his hand under her shift, pushed his hand up inside her, where it was wet. Her sex had been drenched from the moment his thick tongue pushed in her lips. She wished his scarlet tongue were where his hand was, though at the same time she did not want it taken away from its wet swollen probing in her mouth. Stop, she thought, as his tongue traced circles in her mouth, painful circles she could feel all the way down in her groin. She wanted the young man to stick his tongue deep inside her, but this was impossible, she realised. Since the man does not live, she thought, as she felt him pushing her skirt up even higher, over her hips.

She tore herself free and stared at him as they sat there on the leaves. A lovely venom was firing through her lower body but she told herself to calm down. Then he spoke; she hadn't suspected that he would speak. His voice was low and came out slowly, but his words were precise. His expression was knowing. And, though his cock was thick and hard, he did not seem flustered in the slightest. She swallowed nervously; she felt sure she looked far less relaxed.

'You weren't supposed to kiss me; you got it wrong,' he said, tapping one finger against his dimpled cheek and looking at her, his eyes running down her body. The poison swam inside her. 'We'll have to change the story now, of course; it's not how it was meant to be. We'll say I kissed you instead.'

'But that's not what happened.' She looked around her, but in the woods there was only her and the pale red-haired man.

'But it will sound much better that way, won't it? You sleep lifeless in the woods, pale and beautiful, with the source of poison near your lips to indicate how your death occurred. Not the mistletoe, no, that's too obvious. Something red and pretty, to match the colour on your lips. An apple. A poisoned red apple.'

'I would never eat a poisoned apple.' She stole an indirect look at his sex. His hair there grew tightly in copper curls. She wanted to finger and pull out the spirals.

'No?' His smirk told her he had seen her glance. 'But that's not how the story will be told. There will be a demure young woman in soft focus. Passive and soft and just like you – wandering through a picturesque woods. Someone will be jealous of you; someone always is. Do you understand jealousy? You'll be offered presents, secret gifts, bright apples as scarlet as my hair.' He touched himself where she wanted to touch him, buried his hand where her hand should be and stroked himself amidst the soft curls. She understood jealousy. 'That's how the story will be told.'

He got up lazily to lean against a tree, not bothering to stifle a yawn. He was irritatingly handsome with wicked eyes and, despite herself, she grew warm in the pit of her stomach.

She could already feel the poison. She felt her chest tighten and involuntarily her hands began to clench into fists. She was irritated. 'I'm the one who kissed you –' her anger passed quickly and as it abated her voice softened '– I woke you with a kiss, and touched your hair, and –'

'But that's not how it was meant to be.'

'And why not? All the tales I know have men smooching women they think are dead, and no one thinks anything of it and the story goes on from there and – how does it go on? Happily ever after?' she asked suddenly, both sullen and curious. Although she had been told them many times before, she couldn't remember how fairy tales was supposed to end.

'That's the last you ever hear of the couple, usually,' said the young man. 'I don't know about the happily ever after.' He raised one eyebrow and looked straight at her breasts until she began to feel uncomfortable.

'But you're dead,' she said. Her voice was abrupt. 'You were dead, weren't you?'

'Oh, bravo,' said the man. He stretched his body and rubbed his back against the bark of the tree. His hair also rippled against the bark. Her mouth watered with poison. 'Give the girl a medal.'

'How did it happen?' she asked. Her insides were curling and extending, smooth like velvet. 'How did you die?'

He didn't meet her gaze. 'It wasn't how it was meant to be. Someone was jealous.' He twisted his red-gold hair in thought. 'And then I was offered poison. Beautiful mistletoe poison. And then I tasted it.' He fell silent.

'But that's practically the same story as the one you want to tell. Why do you want to change it?'

'Because it's not how the story is meant to be. There are important differences.'

She turned away and picked up her half-full basket and spade to go, but the young man called to her.

'Isn't that right?' he said behind her. She turned around. He grinned at her and ran his eyes over her body, lingering between her legs.

She felt a hot slow flush begin to rise up through her body. 'No, it's not right. Not all the time,' she said. And then, more gently, 'But I could show you how it could be, if you want. I can kiss you, too.' She stepped forward and raked her fingers through the hang of his hair. 'I can kiss you; you don't always have to kiss me first. It doesn't always have to be like that.'

'Now you're teasing.' The beautiful young man smiled. 'But that's all right, that's how it's meant to be. You tease and seduce me; I take you when and if I feel like it.'

She gripped her basket harder. 'I'm just supposed to lie down in the snow and muck and let you have your way with me?'

The red-haired man smiled, his eyes glittering. 'That's why you're the one who should be kissed.'

'What type of person is kissed?'

'Oh, you know – pretty, soft, does what they're told.'

She came up behind him and dropped her basket and spade for the second time that afternoon. She pulled lightly on his hair; it flowed like warm ruby honey past his hips. She gripped him on both cheeks of his arse. She ran one finger over the tight flesh, and then ran it abruptly over the crack of his scarlet-ridged arsehole. She heard a moan from him, a very light moan, and then she knew what she was going to do. She reached around and felt each of his firm balls, weighing them almost gently in her palm, before she pushed him forward until he was on his hands and knees, bent before her. She heard him breathing heavily. She knew she was breathing heavily as well, but as her cunt throbbed she also knew she didn't care what she sounded like.

He, in any case, was silent now. She didn't know if this was how it was meant to be. But she was in it for her pleasure, so she ran another lingering hand across his slender masculine body and raised herself to walk around to face him. Her feet still ached in the slush, but she was beginning to enjoy the sensation – the constant stinging complemented her growing arousal nicely and was a delicious counterpoint. She faced the red-haired man again. His head was bowed, and she raised it up so he could look her in the eyes. She kissed him hard. The sugary poison lingered in her mouth. She was going to get what she wanted.

She let her gaze go down his whole body and his beautiful crimson hair again, just as his gaze had recently scraped over her. He watched her looking, and she read in his expression that it shamed and aroused him. She reached down and took hold of his cock. He was stiff and he shook when she alternated a light pressing with a firm grip. She wasn't going to let him spill yet, though. She released his hard member and knelt in front of him, so that the tips of her breasts were more or less even with his eyes. Her legs were far apart as she knelt, and she slowly reached under her shift and reached up into herself, gripping herself hard. She didn't want this to be easy and soft, the kind of fuck he'd expect from the girl he thought she should be.

The eyes of the red-haired man glazed as he watched her touch herself, and she hitched her skirt up so he could see more clearly. She rolled her finger over the stiff and wet parts of her sex, enjoying the contrasts within her. Her finger lightly circled the little bud, until she grew so hot and trembling she made herself stop. She didn't want this to be over, not quite yet. She took her hand from her sex and thrust it in his mouth, and he sucked at her fingers so confidently and erotically that she felt half-tempted to test his skills elsewhere. But that wasn't what she had in mind for him, either.

'You like that?' she asked him. She removed her hand. 'Do I taste like I ought to?' He nodded, afraid to speak and break the spell of the woods. She had to feel herself quickly once more; she rubbed her hand once across her cunt and the feeling of sex rippled up through her. She could smell sex everywhere – on him and on her, and she didn't want to wait anymore.

She walked with slow precision around behind the red-haired man; she didn't want to seem as if she was hurrying. She ran a hand under his body as she walked, from the sweat on his neck to his hard nipples, to the muscular furrow of his navel, all the way down to his hard cock. He was not insisting on keeping to the story now, she observed, and she felt both smug and horny. He didn't make a sound. She looked at him again from behind, the delicious sight of his splayed arse and the straining hollows of his hips. She stuck a finger up herself again and then spread her wetness over his hole, oiled his slender buttocks open for her and for her alone.

The moaning started again – but she realised it was her, this time. She couldn't wait to get started. He twitched forward and she gave him a light slap on one cheek. 'You're not coming before I am.' She picked up the spade from where she had dropped it previously and untwisted its wooden dowel-like handle, discarding the blade itself on the ground. The sun was even stronger on her neck and shoulders and she was beginning to think of it as an aphrodisiac. She could smell the ripe moss of the woods and she could smell the sex between her and the red-haired man.

She continued to make him wet with her own lubrication; she lavished his arsehole with her wetness. Then she reached forward and pressed on his upper back, so that he bent down with only his pretty arse in the air for her to feel and see. She stroked it admiringly several times, but then remembered exactly what her intentions were. She pushed the smooth dowel into his arse, and it was tight, so tight around the dowel that she felt her cunt tighten, too, as if the slick dowel were inside her as well. She gripped him by his hair and began fucking him slowly and, when he put his hand back to touch himself, she decided benevolently to let him. She liked the thought of him wanking while the smooth dowel entered and re-entered his arse, wet from her sex.

Sweet Poison

She made the dowel move slightly faster, and both she and the red-haired man were breathing heavily; they were in pace with each other. 'But I'm coming first, mind you,' she hissed at him and stopped the movement of the dowel momentarily as a little warning. He pushed himself back on to it. 'If you're wanting more,' she said, 'I'll do you with pleasure. Happily.' She still didn't move the dowel. But she knew in herself that his eagerness excited her, so she redoubled her efforts with the smooth wood, running her free hand through his beautiful hanging red-blond hair. 'Happily ever after,' she added, the tattoo beating a frenzy into him.

She couldn't wait; she pushed him flat on his stomach and climbed astride him. She mounted the protruding end of the dowel in his beautiful arse and rode it, circling her fingers hard through her slippery sex. She came and it was absolutely delicious; she gripped the waves of red-gold hair as it hit her, and she rolled into the boy, and all she saw was red and all she tasted was red and it was sweet poison in her body and she loved it.

She got up. She was staring at the prone body of a young man with long red-gold hair, lying on his back. Her unsevered spade was in her hand, along with her basket. The red-haired man lay calmly on a bed of green leaves, as if waiting for someone to wake him with a kiss. She stroked his cheek and turned to go, but she bent to pick up a piece of a dark green plant with pearlised berries. She would have to leave the woods; it was going to be getting dark soon. But before she let the plant drop from her hand, she ran her tongue once along the edge of a single white berry and felt the tingling in her mouth. She knew it was poison, but it was so sweet. She wouldn't let its nectar get the better of her, though. That's not how it was meant to be.

Frozen Violets

Frozen Violets

In Northern lands there has always been a tale whispered, one in which a brother and a sister leave their cruel family and follow a trail deep, deep into the woods. There, it is said, they find a fantastic house, and in it a witch. This story is older than it seems, for in the eleventh century in the cold Viking mountains the tale was already being told. The siblings were already present in this early rendering of the legend, as was the strange house in the woods. There was an evil stepparent; a trail that the siblings followed through the forest. But the story then was not how people whisper it now, made careful and safe in the retelling. The old story was more curious, the story of how Oshu and Ola once met Skathi, the Norse goddess who lived alone in the hills to track and hunt.

It is the story of how a brother and sister left a warm house to escape a cruel father, and then were alone in the bleak landscape of the Scandinavian mountains, two figures moving between the blue shadows cast by the trees on the cream-white snow. The sister had huge black eyes that were serious and thoughtful; full, lush lips and ebony skin so dark it shone nearly purple in the starlight. Her tight-curled hair was woven into an inky rope of braid, intertwined with threads of silver and gold. She had once been a rich man's daughter, and beneath the rough foreign furs and cloths she wore a small amethyst tucked into her navel. She thought of it

Astrid Fox

as a secret; a reminder of the life she had before she came to this cold land. She was the older of the two, proud and confident and brave.

Her brother was fairer in skin but just as beautiful. His eyes were green; his hair loose curls that skimmed his neck. He was seventeen. In this barren country, thought his sister, people counted time by cycles of seasons rather than by shifting alternations of rain and drought and it seemed a crude process to her. She did not like it.

They had a mother in common.

At first, they moved quickly through the snow, but when they realised that they were not being followed they stopped to catch their breath. It was then that the brother noticed the trail. Now they stood nearly immobile, their leather-bound feet just breaking through the first crisp layer of snow. Over them the sky trembled out patterns of weird colours; it looked to the girl as if the whole sky were transforming to an ocean: surely the wavering blues and greens in the heavens were found by rights within the slippery panorama of the sea. The sister lowered her eyes from the sight. It was not the first thing that she had found disturbing in this land to which their mother had brought them; not the first sight that had disconcerted her.

She turned to her brother and said, not for the first time, 'So let's follow this trail; see where it goes.'

'Yes.' The brother looked out over the mounds of snow behind them, in front of them, to both sides of them.

She wondered whether his back still stung from his father's beating of the day before, and wondered if he knew that it had been worse for her. Still, here was the trail strung out before them, an escape of some sorts. And yes, it has been her brother who had first picked up one of the objects that had made up the trail and shown it to her. It was a frozen petal of a flower she had not yet seen in this country, but she had recognised it immediately as the petal of a violet.

Frozen Violets

He had lain the purple chip in her hand, its colour in stark contrast to her light palm. She had raised her hand and licked at its flat glassy surface; felt its fragile structure crumble at the warmth from her tongue. For just a moment then, she had felt that her brother was watching her intently, strangely. But that was before the two of them had noticed a whole line of frozen violet petals dotted through the snow, leading into the curve of the white forest. Evidence, it seemed, that someone else was near. Perhaps someone who could help them.

They began to walk again. They followed the trail of frozen violets, which looked like a line of bruises on the snow. The girl thought of the bruises on her brother's arms, and she winced. It had been her idea to leave; had been she who had gathered food and clothes and woken him while her mother and stepfather lay sleeping. The whole time they had crept out she had been afraid of the assault that would follow if her brother's father woke, but she had whispered a prayer and they had left him sleeping in the house.

The moon and stars made things look eerie in the now pale, now blue woods; the shadows were more violent and sharp-edged against the white snow. And her brother's face was even more haunting: delicate, beautiful, wistful; lashes juxtaposed like black feathers against his heavy lids as his eyes moved to survey the dark forest. She cleared her throat, reached for her brother's covered hand and they passed by trees piled with blankets of sparkling, dustlike snow.

She was bitter. She had been betrayed by only one parent, but he had been betrayed by both. She had been right to suggest that they leave. No more beatings, no more excuses mouthed by their ashamed and weak mother, so hopelessly in love with her husband that she ignored her own children.

'The trail continues here,' the girl told her brother, showing him how the petals led between the overladen branches of pine, through the papery frozen skins of the cold birch trees.

The girl was turning cold now; it felt like her skin was freezing painfully from the inside. Her cheeks were no longer cold – just numb skin over the chilled blood beneath. Even the amethyst was growing cold, a frigid pit caught deep in the indentation in her abdomen. She did not wish to alarm her brother, but she feared that they would have to return if they did not soon find the source of this trail. It had to be a human and not an animal; to leave a trail of frozen petals seemed a particularly human thing to do. She shivered, remembering how her stepfather had told them tales of the angry Northern gods even before he had taken them north by treks and sea.

It was then that they saw the house.

They stopped in shock, their feet sinking into the snow. At the same time as she felt relief, the girl's heart sank. For here was warmth and shelter, but here was also what was obviously the abode of one of the Northern gods of whom her father had spoken.

The house was between two arcing pines and the trails stopped right at its door. She had not yet seen such a wondrous sight in this cold, ugly land and, thirsty for beauty, her eyes were drawn to its details. When she could not explain the coloured ice, her mind made up explanations for her: in place were blocks of frozen crimson wine, crystallised rivers of green-gold honey and purple blueberry juice suspended in the frozen house. She whispered this explanation to her brother, and for him it was enough that his sister offered a cause for the colours; he did not question further until he pointed to the fruits embedded in the ice, dotted along the ice house.

'What are these?'

The girl scoured her imagination for answers. 'Sweetmeats of raspberries,' she told him, 'strawberries, orange *hjortron* berries placed at the ends of the eaves.'

Frozen Violets

'Why does the house shine?'

'It is the thousand candles from within the house that makes it glow with colour and light.' It could be the truth, she told herself. She looked long at the ice house, and held her brother's hand tightly. Her mind kept on explaining silently: the house was yellow where pine pitch had been swirled into the ice; glowing sun-coloured spirals decorated with small flowers: blue forget-me-nots, little buds of roses just kissed with scarlet, the separated petals of dandelions. It was as if a summer garden had been caught, preserved within the house itself. When she had arrived in summer, she had thought the Norse flowers small and inadequate, but that was before winter had come and there were none at all.

'What is it?' said her brother.

The girl knew very well that it was one of the houses of the Northern gods, but she was reluctant to let her brother know that – he would be able to tell that she was frightened.

'I'm not sure,' she said.

'Can I touch it?'

She watched silently as her brother began to circle the house of light, running his hands against its melting sides, licking at its honey-coloured walls, his hands flat against the structure. The girl watched him do this; she could almost feel the wetness on her own palms. They could not return now; they would freeze to death in the attempt, and so she must gather courage and knock on the door of the angry Northern god. She wondered if the god would be as terrible as the people of this land had been, whether he would laugh and scorn her beautiful dark skin. She would spit at him and leave, she decided, if that happened. Even if it meant her death in the snow. She was too tired of the cold country and its cruel people.

She pushed open the door, and saw with relief that there was no angry male god, but rather a naked woman who sat at a hearth whose fire burned and licked and curled red flame, lighting the house inside as well as outside.

'There are no thousand candles,' her brother whispered behind her, but she ignored him.

The pale woman stood up. She had short hair, and she was nearly tall as a man. She had a strange necklace round her throat of small twigs that were fused together in the shapes that these Northern people called runes, and the woman fingered them slowly as she spoke. 'Where have you come from?'

'From far away,' the boy answered. His sister would have gestured for him not to speak, but he seemed enthralled by the woman. The girl knew, however, that it was dangerous to speak to strangers. She waited for the inevitable questions as to their origin and the questions as to the colour of their skin. She didn't want to tell the same story all over again, of how her Nigerian mother had met her Viking stepfather in the distant trading lands to the south and then borne a son to the Northern stranger. The girl felt angry when she thought of how her stepfather had forced her mother north, and only grudgingly permitted his new wife to take her children: a daughter from a previous marriage and a half-Northern son. Relating the familiar information made the girl tired; it would be the same questions, the same clucking disapproval.

But the short-haired woman was quiet for a moment, touching her twig necklace, and merely looked sad. 'I, too, come from far away,' she said, and then fell silent.

'From where?' the boy prompted. His sister wanted to shake him for being so forward; it had earnt him many a beating in the past. Who knew what this strange Northern woman was capable of?

'The land of the frost giants,' said the woman, and the girl felt a chill run up her spine as she recalled again her stepfather's stories. 'But that was long ago,' the woman added. 'Long ago and far away.' She looked piercingly at the siblings, each in turn.

The girl felt herself go hot despite the snow piled in layers on

Frozen Violets

her clothing. She knew who the woman was, and she and her brother should leave right now if they were to be saved from her clutches. Yes, she knew the story from her stepfather; this woman was the solitary goddess in a house of ice. The girl cursed herself for having ignored the clues to the woman's identity. The woman was still looking at her, straight in her eyes. They had to go now. Now. She turned to her brother, but he was smiling at the woman, and the girl felt her heart sink. They were lost. She would never be able to convince her brother to leave to a sure death in the snow.

'You're wet and cold,' the ice woman observed. 'Take off your clothes and draw close to the fire.'

The girl hung back, watching as her brother did as the Northern woman asked, as if he were hypnotised by her voice. She watched him take off the soaked bright woollen shirt and reveal his taut stomach; and the youthful, wiry muscles of his arms, and she also watched the woman's pale blue eyes grow bright. The ice woman saw what she herself saw: that her brother was a beautiful man. He kept his trousers on. The girl closed her eyes and swallowed.

'You, too.' The woman's voice was low and persuasive.

The girl kept her eyes closed, hearing the crackle of the fire and the breath of both her brother and the woman. Finally she sighed, reasoning that if they were doomed it was better to be dry and warm. She stripped, revealing her high breasts and hips, still as slim as a youth's. She thought she saw the woman's eyes shining as they had before. The girl joined her half-brother before the fire, crouching low and feeling the heat on her chest and throat. Her brother laid a hand on her neck and stroked her there, as if in reassurance. Perhaps he was right. Perhaps she had no cause yet to be suspicious.

The ice woman's voice broke in. She was standing some distance behind them, evidently still observing them. 'My name is Skathi.' It was a statement; it did not seem that she was asking for a similar revelation from them.

A moment passed, and the girl felt her toes grow warm again as they began to unthaw. Her brother removed his hand from his sister's neck, and the girl sensed that he was hurt; that he did not understand her rudeness to the woman. It's not rudeness, she thought, just caution. But nothing yet had happened in the house of ice, nothing like that her stepfather had warned her about. Her stepfather had said that Skathi cracked the bones of children with her teeth and drank the blood of men. That Skathi had come from the land of the giants; had married one of the Northern gods and then left him behind, in order to live alone in the mountains where she hunted and skied on skis formed from long antlers and ate disobedient children – and even disobedient young women, her stepfather had added. Skathi lived in a house of ice and could never go home. She was banished from the gods, and banished from her own people, the giants, as well.

She heard her brother sigh beside her; she knew that he would not speak again until she herself had said it was all right. The amethyst in her navel began to grow warm once more.

'Oshu and Ola,' she finally said, pointing to herself and her half-brother in turn. She gave the Norse approximations. She didn't tell the stranger their real names; it was not a gift she would willingly bestow upon a stranger. She stretched her fingers out before the fire and did not look behind her. Already she regretted speaking.

'Oshu,' the woman said, and the girl heard her approach from behind. The woman put her hand on her bare shoulder, and the girl shut her eyes for the death blow that was coming – but it did not happen. Skathi's hand felt soft and safe, as her brother's hand had felt. 'Oshu,' the ice woman said again, 'what brings you here? Why is there such pain in you?'

The girl turned around to face the woman, goddess or not. Her own eyes were filled to the brim with tears, and she could only imagine what her brother was thinking. He had never seen her cry. 'I never wanted to be here.' She stared at the pale woman, as

Frozen Violets

if daring her to deny it.

'Nor did I,' the goddess – if that was what she was – said softly. She stepped closer, and the girl saw that her eyes were kind. For a moment she wanted only to succumb; she was tired of holding in all the exhausting pain, tired of being the strong one for both her brother and herself. Out of the corner of her eye, she saw her brother watching silently; saw his skin shining in the light from the fire. Then she exhaled, eyes closed. A single tear ran down her cheek. Then she leant forward, nearly fell into the woman's pale arms.

The Northern woman ran her hand down her braid, and for a moment the girl shuddered, remembering how her Viking stepfather used to yank at it. She was away from that now, she told herself. Skathi put her lips to the dark girl's throat, cool skin against cool skin, and licked a warm trail down to the sculptural frame of the girl's shoulderblades and collarbone. The girl was briefly and desperately reminded of the trail they had followed, and wondered if they would ever claw their way out again. But heat was surging through her, heat that she hadn't felt since the day her mother had forced them on their journey north. She was reminded of home: the rich scent of vividly coloured flowers, of bright laughter and brilliant sun.

'You remember your home,' the woman whispered in her ear, and the girl knew then that she was indeed a goddess, or at the very least a priestess, able to see what was in a person's heart.

Yes, she thought, I remember. But Skathi drew away, and left the girl standing on the furs covering the earth floor of the ice house, pondering how her memory of home had suddenly flared back now, after so many months in this cold, ugly land.

Her mouth was dry, and she was aware that there was wetness between her legs. And now this strange woman was doing the same to her brother, kissing a gentle track down his skin; and the girl watched how her brother shut his eyes, clenching his hands into fists at his side; watched how the swelling at his groin grew beneath the alien clothes that they both hated.

'Ola,' Skathi said, and whispered something in his ear. He licked his lips, and his sister trembled with emotion. Her brother was beautiful. She felt a light sweat beading on her body, and irrationally wondered whether the tall cold woman would notice. She watched as the woman ran her hands over the displaced cloth below her brother's waist, stroking and caressing at the hardness that the girl knew was there. This seemed safe and right and the icy room was bright and hot. The girl thought that she could smell the sweet, heavy scent of living violets, all the way from home.

Her breath was coming quicker now as she watched the woman, naked except for the necklace of twigs, leaning over her brother. The girl pressed a hand against her crotch and a sweet sensation began to stir there, so she rubbed her fingers roughly up between her legs. She kept her eyes on her brother and the strange white woman. His trousers were being removed now as well. She couldn't help her jealousy: what if the woman were to touch her like her brother was being touched; to stroke her softly between her legs? Would she like it, or would she feel frightened?

The fire crackled higher. There was a scent of musk in the air, and the girl slipped her hand down to feel the curls of her own sex-hair. She pushed down a finger into the stickiness there, the sticky warmth she had felt gathering ever since the woman had licked at the flesh of her throat. She pressed down on her little bud and moaned; when she opened her eyes seconds later, her finger still on the bud of her sex, both the woman and her brother were staring at her. To her surprise she felt no shame whatsoever, and held their gazes while she continued to move her finger, slipping over the hard little centre of her sex. All around her was the heady fragrance of violets.

'Come,' said the woman called Skathi, and she motioned them down to the rug of fur spread out over the whole of the ice-house

Frozen Violets

floor. The woman laid herself down on the rug, stomach against the dark pelt.

Both siblings stared at her, and then at each other. The girl's pulse was racing wildly in her breast, and she saw her brother's excitement from his hard cock, thick and ready, jutting from his young body. If I were a man too, she thought, I would look like that. Ready. I feel ripe, ripe as violets in bloom. She ran her hands up over her stiff nipples. She felt tight all over, as if her skin was too small for her body. Her brother was still looking at her, but neither moved, as if they were afraid to move either closer down to the woman on the rug, or closer to each other. Then all at once her brother reached for her, and she felt his breath before his wet, slow kiss, and she felt desire rising up through her as he held her, his arms tight around her. There was the scent of violets in his curls, she noticed, and for a moment they both forgot about the woman Skathi as they lost themselves in the kiss.

But the girl broke the kiss eventually, breathless, and stared down at the short-haired woman, who was watching them intently but still, it seemed, patiently. When the ice woman saw that they were both staring at her, she moaned gently, and just the sound of it sent a thrill through the girl. She felt just like the Northern woman, as if she were lazy and creamily wet, so ready and ripe. She was not surprised when her brother stepped forward to the Northern woman; indeed, if he had not, she would have done so herself.

The fire, she noticed, was making the walls of the ice house run, but nothing about either heat nor cold could scare her now, as she watched her brother slowly kissing the white woman's haunches, the curve of her arse, and rubbing his fingers in the valley between her legs. He raised his hand, and his sister could see it shimmering with wetness, then he licked at it and sucked at the moisture, and this time both women moaned at the same time.

The girl found herself walking closer, around to the front of the woman, and she crouched before the Northerner, her thighs on either side of the woman's head. The woman's face was flushed, and she moaned again. The girl saw that her brother had entered the woman from behind, his cock forging deep into her, and the girl heard the wet sounds as it entered the woman: sloppy, lusty sounds. She thought of her brother's beauty, and she felt her face grow hot again.

'Oshu.' The woman murmured her name, and ran her hands along the younger woman's thighs. 'Come closer, Oshu.'

The girl shut her eyes; the overpowering scent of ripe violets stinging through her head, and moved her wet crotch closer to the stranger, then slowly opened her legs to her. The woman began to lap at her, at first gently, and then the ice woman was lustily drinking from her, as the girl's brother pumped into the woman from behind. The girl was nervous at first, but then pleasure began to pound through her from the woman's mouth, and eventually she fell back, the woman continuing to lap, and her brother continued to fuck the woman, his hands on the woman's limber athletic legs, and the girl smelled violets everywhere, violets and her own ripe arousal, the scent swirling together in the musk of perfume. She was blind to the other two, though, as the pleasure tightened and then exploded though her, as she shoved her sex down against the woman's mouth, the woman's face glistening with juices. The woman was also bucking, her hand down on her own sex as the girl's brother lunged and then finally withdrew, his pearly, salty come sprayed over the woman's buttocks and thighs. The woman continued to move her hand against her sex and lick deep inside the girl, and she groaned deeply as she reached her climax.

They lay there together, panting for a long while, the girl listening to the ice house drip from the heat of the fire. Then Skathi moved, got up and quickly clothed herself in furs. 'Come,' she said, and helped them dress and don a pair of skis each, as she did herself. The house was melting quickly.

Frozen Violets

'I don't want to return to my mother and my stepfather,' the girl said, knowing that she must assert herself quickly, as it looked as if the woman was getting ready to lead them away.

'Nor I,' her brother quickly added, his face still glowing with excitement. He said it in the tone of one who felt it necessary to break at last from a beloved sibling and find his own voice, the girl noted with a touch of sadness.

'No,' said Skathi, ushering them quickly out before the house began to crash in on itself. She stretched out a hand to each and led them to a sled, which was fastened by sinew to a great elk. The snow was beginning to fall softly and the girl looked behind to the melting spectacle of the ice house, now crumpled into a mass of coloured ice blocks and frozen flowers, covered by the gentle flakes of snow spinning slowly from the grey sky.

For once her brother moved without his sister's approval, climbing up into the sled, a sled which was piled high with furs. He pulled his sister up into the curving frame, and they nestled amongst the furs, warm and safe. Snow melted on the girl's long lashes. The liquid blurred her vision for a moment, but then she saw Skathi throw herself up on the huge horned beast and give out a piercing whistle. The sled began to grate against the rocks beneath the snow, before it hit its glide on the cool white drifts.

The girl held her brother's hand tightly as the elk began to race. The sled went faster and faster down the hill, pulled by the beast, until even the blue, drift-covered trees became a haze before the girl's dark eyes. The speed was so tremendous that she and her brother shut their lids against the slash of the cold wind but, just as they had done so, the sled abruptly stopped.

The sister and brother opened their eyes. In the air was a searing, beautiful, sexual scent of wild violets, and she still held her brother's hand tightly. It was clear morning, a beautiful winter day. They sat within the heaps of furs lining the sled, but both Skathi and the great elk had melted away; the sled's sinew leads dangled limply in the snow, unattached.

Up ahead there was a village and the girl knew that they would be able to get board there and eat before continuing their long voyage home. For a moment she tried to remember home, her true home: bright sun and palm trees. But behind her she could still sense the presence of the lonely goddess, perhaps watching from the woods.

'Look,' the girl's brother said to his sister before he climbed down from the bowl of the sled, 'she's left us food as well.' He had been looking through the furs, and now his hands were cupped full of the same summer fruits that had decorated the house of ice, scooped up from a pile at their feet: the same fresh berries and edible flowers. For the first time in a long while, the girl saw hope upon her brother's face.

The girl thought for a moment before she climbed down and began the trek to the village, trying to understand the witchery that had brought them both safely here. She tried to remember the burning hearth, the woman's thin, slightly bitter but kind smile, her short hair. She tried to visualise the house they had escaped from in the first place, but it already seemed to be solely a bad dream. The only image she could summon was the trail of violet petals, but in her vision they were no longer frozen chips but soft and tender; bruised, but still alive.

This is the older story, and it is the truer one, as well.

The Curie Quandary

The Curie Quandary

The long nights in the laboratory.

It was the intimacy of those moments, the odd seclusion of so many intent hours, working in the near-twilight of the shed. The hours peering at those glowing metals, metals that she would drift off to sleep and dream about: green and beautiful, glowing like fireflies, like the swamp gas she had heard of. She would stare at these compounds at night sometimes, stare and think of his long pale hands. His breath on her neck, his voice low in her ear as she bent over her ciphers. She wished that he would reach out then, reach out one of those pale fingers and touch the tendril escaping from her chignon. Yes, her hair was damp during summer days and summer evenings, but she never looked up, not in those days. Her hands would shake as she wrote out long scrawls in her copperplate writing, thinking, go away, you must go away. And after a while he would. And she would stay in her laboratory, bury her head in her hands and continue to shake. Her legs, trembling between her long, sombre skirts. Her throat constricting. Her gusset damp. She would scribble then for hours into the night, willing herself to calculate. The radiated metal would glow like soft luminous plants, sculptures of lamps. She wanted him, even then. She could not tell her husband.

I am also a scientist. So I am an objective woman, and I look formally at previous examples in order to learn, myself.

Oh yes, like the Curies, I sit there with my husband and him, too, supping the same meals, swallowing soup that turns still hotter in my throat when our eyes meet. There is tension at our table. There is cool milk swallowed; there are my excuses to leave the room so I do not have to see his soft blue eyes, mild under the spectacles, avoiding mine, as frightened of meeting my gaze as I am of meeting his. But unlike the Curies, I have the gift of her example. She also kept silent, I imagine. She loved her husband, very much, so her grief when he died made it worse, as if she had called it up by her laboratory wishes. She was only 38, you know. And then five years later, Madame won the Prize for the second time.

His presence makes me think of old words, words I haven't thought of since my husband and I first were courting, so it must be three or four years since the power of those words has hit me. Crude and vulgar words. It is said, but not confirmed, that he has a sweetheart, I overheard someone gossiping the fact in the market only last week, and I find myself thinking of them together sometimes.

The year now, of course, is 1913, and the world is shifting into war, and two years have passed since Madame's great scandal with her colleague. There are other women scientists; I have more examples, though we are tiny in number, all of us. In twenty years, perhaps, we will not struggle as Marie, and I, and the others have done. When we make our applications, the Academies will not vote on our sex but on our minds. Soon, if the efforts of Mrs Pankhurst and her daughters and many others prove true, we will vote on law here in England. So that is something. That is a great thing. The world may be violent but it is changing, and we help it change, we bring light to the darkness – new methods, new equations, new explanations.

I write out my own equations at night, as Madame did. Sometimes I think of the scholar named Mr Perrin, whose research

The Curie Quandary

indicates that the atoms of which we are built are themselves like planetary systems, the subparticles circling just as our Earth circles the Sun. All this circling, our huge planet, our tiny building blocks, no action, pulled by gravity, never touching. Eventually it makes my head spin, too, and I have to cry. I always wash my face before I join my husband in our bed and he does not know my struggle.

Eventually, I become aware of a scenario that plays itself out in my head like an excerpt from a banned, risqué novel: I just want to see his face when he reaches the peak of pleasure. I am not sure whether I am particularly attracted to this man, save in a cerebral sense. But there is something I find deeply stirring and even, yes, appealing, intriguing, about him, if one can feel all that without technically wanting the act of intimate congress with a person, and the sentiment would still be named attraction.

I am a lady scientist. I am a cool thinker, not a feverish muddle of emotion like other members of my sex. I believe that women have the capacity for rationality, if only we are indulged and permitted. I record my notes patiently. I, too, like Madame, study in a garden shed with a supportive, brilliant husband and an additional male, the colleague who boards with us.

So I look at the whole situation as an equation itself. In my head, where no one can test my evidence, proofs and conclusions, I have laughingly labelled it the Curie Quandary. I wonder, did she act on her feelings for the blue-eyed man, even while she loved and desired her husband? I think probably she did not.

All three of them worked together. She and the blue-eyed man taught together. The blue-eyed man had even been a student of her husband's. It was only later, when she was already a widow and he was so unhappy in his own marriage, that matters changed. Circumstantial, not essential. Had matters been different, had Marie's husband Pierre lived, for instance, the choices Madame made would have also been different. This is what I think happened. That is how it works, in this equation.

Astrid Fox

Here is what I desire, what I think would be particularly sensual. It is probably most truly an act of mental amusement, a game. A supposition, not a quandary. It does not involve a congress between ourselves. But it does involve each of us being aware of the other's presence, a knowingness, like a very subtle, very sweet poison. I would like to see him with his sweetheart, in all their intimacy. I'd like to see her hand round his hardness. I would like him to know that I was watching them; I would want to know that my watching would make him even stiffer. There is something perverse about the whole matter, as I said, it involves being there and not being there, being in someone's mind and not being in someone's mind; I think it is about openness and partitions, the points where you realise that it must be time to stop letting someone into your dreams anymore, the odd feeling when you know you've poisoned someone else in the same way, you're convinced of it, you feel it, you don't need proof.

And it's not proper poison, just a shade of it, not even close to what you feel for your husband, and it's not love and it's not exactly carnal, it's a bit too uncomfortable for friendship (but it could evolve to a true friendship at some point if you are both very, very careful and very, very respectful), it's the shadow of what-could-have-been, the shade of what-could-have-been, in a different universe, on a different planet, circling round different atoms, in a different lifetime.

Sci-fi Cliché #10

Sci-fi Cliché #10

At first, all he could see was blue.

The palace rose up like a hunk of sky in the grey horizon: ostentatious. It was the first thing he noticed. Its windows were smog-coloured, as closed to the world outside as dead computer monitors. But the frosty blue marble of the palace framed these windows like the sky framed clouds. It was impossible to ignore magnificence of this order; impossible to ignore the odd beauty of extremity. Splendour: the silver trim of the bulwarks that ran up the sides of the palace like silver icicles. Splendour: the 7,000 lights imbedded in the walls. There, these lamps glittered like neon stars. They crackled with sharp energy. They snapped into 7,000 electric-blue flares. They clicked off again.

The heavens above the castle were upstaged, but received high marks for effort. They moved silver, grey, icy white; two suns winking out their cool rays. For a human, it was impossible not to be moved by the castle, but these inhuman globes gleamed like twinned robin's eggs, pale and perfect and nonchalant in the slate-coloured sky. Suns do not have the responsibility to explain their world to foreigners who walk upon its surface. Click, went the palace lights. Click, click. Sascha felt the wind begin to blow as he walked forward, air forcing its way into his mouth as he inhaled. Cold. Menthol. It was already winter on the alien world.

He kept walking slowly towards the castle. The craft, the metal-lined trap and saviour of a ship that had borne him here, was behind him, crushed in a snowless landscape coloured mist-grey; coloured like those ancient marks Sascha's ancestors made on paper: grey and then grey again, pencil-lead scratchings of grey language on white fibrous sheets, grey graphite, grey as the smoke that rose from cold lakes in the morning, grey and then grey again.

He would walk all the way up to the castle. All the way up to the doorstep he could now see looming in front of him. He would march up to the castle and seek out its tenants, and then he would either be killed or, with their help, begin to look for Severn.

There was a soundtrack that accompanied his steps towards the great blue architecture whose seven-grand lamps twinkled like a circuitboard: he felt like he were about to walk inside an ancient computer. The building seemed devoid of organic life; it buzzed and crackled with the energy of a machine. And this music which surrounded him, this eerie, rather high-pitched music, was not sourced from the palace. It came from the air, from the shadowy ground. Perhaps speakers were implanted in the earth and the melody that rose up was caught invisible in the air, caught in an oxygen net. For surely enough it was oxygen that he breathed here on the alien world, sweet familiar oxygen that had filled his lungs after his ship fell from the sky and the helmet had been torn from his head on impact.

The lights flickered. Click, they said.

The marble rose up in blue sheets a mile above his head when he looked up. He had reached the doorstep.

Click.

He walked through this open hole in the wall, and then he was in a long hallway. The music ceased immediately; he was right, it had come from the outdoors. The lights that had illuminated the castle from the outside were not as apparent now; they had also stopped their clicking. The lamps and their circles of dull blue light were only smudges as he walked nervously down the hallway, which wound deeper and more tightly into what had to be the heart of the castle. Yet there were no other options to his path; this was no maze with choices right or wrong; this was only a single path that coiled towards the building's interior, leading him to a destiny which would itself be ill or good. This disturbed him; he was a strong believer in options.

Now Sascha noticed that the marbled rock from which the structure was carved seemed moist, pliant, nearly vegetable. No circuitboard castle now, after all; no neutered automatons lived here. Of course, because the castle could not have grown itself; it was a construction, wasn't it? Sascha shivered, and his skin prickled with fear. Aliens always seemed freakish to him. He never knew what they were thinking. After all, machines and robots do not have the malice or favours of flesh: they might kill, but it is not personal.

There was light ahead, not twinkling lamps but the proverbial light at the end of his tunnel, and Sascha wondered whether he ought to call out or maybe follow local etiquette and sing a soft high melody himself, so as not to sneak up unawares. Then he turned the last corner of the tunnel, and his mouth went dry, and he could not sing.

The whole thing was hollowed out, all the way up to the turrets. It was a gigantic shell of a room once you reached this interior. And maybe the castle was higher than he had even realised, maybe it even pierced past the cloud layer, because the top of the room, when he strained his neck from tilting it back to see how far up the walls went – well, the top was open. Sunlight shot down from this oversized skylight, straight down to the grey grass which made up the floor of this room. Sascha questioned why he persisted in thinking of it as a castle, but knew he did it instinctively, because of its fantastic appearance. It was like an odd kind of zoo, with its zoned-in version of nature; the sunlight and grass were striking, extremely unusual in an enclosed space. These details were not the most remarkable part of the room.

Oh, and the huge river that ran across the great floor, of course. Sascha stared, open-mouthed. It was a quite natural-looking river – it probably *was* a natural river – and one that flowed from one end of the great room to the other, diagonally, away to his right. The sunlight glittered and glistered on the pull of the water, turning it aqua and even the translucent light blue of Perspex plastic. It was stunning. This was also not the most remarkable part of the castle interior.

The most remarkable part of the castle interior was the gathering of two-legged, bald blue creatures of roughly his own height, of roughly his own features and – aside from the three small but fully developed breasts – of roughly his composition. They were bathing in the river or sunning in the clear white sunlight on the grey grass or just standing around – in alarmingly relaxed bipedal stances – chatting. Or at least he guessed it was chatting. Goddamn.

He couldn't believe what he was seeing, and drew closer. All of the triple-breasted females stood or squatted near the river, exposing their greyish-blue hides to the rays of the suns that beamed across the water. The whole scenario evoked a pastoral scene from his own home of Earth, one where animals drank and cooled themselves in rivers. But these blue-skinned aliens were not animals, or at least they were different kinds of animals. He drew even closer. The light reflected off their greyish-blue skin, their dolphin-like skin.

The suns on their hides made them flicker briefly into several other shades of blue. Yes, the sheen of their flesh glittered neon-blue, glacial blue, except for what Sascha saw now as one creature squatted in front of him: he saw the pornographic, close-up genitals of the alien – pink, bubble-gum pink. A sex sticky with

Sci-fi Cliché #10

thick juice, with white creamy come. He felt himself stiffen as he gazed at the alien as she squatted, her back to him, her thighs revealing a flash of pink colour amongst all that blue. A pink that was both lurid and obscene.

It wasn't just their trio of small, tapered blue breasts. Judging by their nether regions, they were all, without exception, female.

Now that he was close enough, he realised that his first impression had been wrong. They didn't seem to be chatting or even talking. They made no sounds at all from those wide blue lips, not even a hum. Nor was there any music here, as there had been outside. The only sound was the roll and babble of the river. He found the quiet, natural warble strangely comforting.

He didn't know why he did the next thing. It wasn't like he was attracted to aliens, or anything. Maybe it was the sight of the cold blue river because, let's face it, he could use a bath. Though he was man enough to admit that the sight of the cool blue aliens with their perversely compelling nether regions made him want to strip off. Maybe it was just because he wanted to be equals with them, naked just like them, only without the supernumerary nipple.

Yeah, that had to be it.

Yet when one of them walked towards him, he flinched. She didn't slow her pace, but continued until she stood only several centimetres away and stared him in the face. He was acutely aware of his nakedness, of the heap of his clothes behind him on the grass, clothes that offered no protection now at all. It had been a mistake to take them off.

She was staring at him. He shifted his arm, but didn't yet move it. Her skin looked as smooth as a dolphin's. He wasn't sure if he wanted to touch the blue-grey flesh, even just to brush the tips of his fingers against her skin to feel its texture. What if it were clammy? What if she didn't want his strokings? Sascha risked it. He reached out and put a finger on her arm. It was cool, not clammy; organic but shelled, like the epidermis of an aubergine or an unripe pear. Or even a pupa: the steely grey sheen to the blue was that of a cocoon. He suppressed an impulse to tap on her arm, beckoning out the insect. He kept his finger where it was. But there was the sensation of warmth below, where her blood ran. Maybe it was blue blood, too. Still, she was no royal: she had the immediacy of the uncrowned common herd. She might be blue, but she was alive and she was breathing in her frosty breath as much as he was breathing out the same air in icy puffs himself. Cool blue. Ice blue. Grey eyes.

They drew him in, those grey eyes. Her hands cradled his head. He sunk lower, lower, down to one of her three breasts. What was he doing? He found he didn't care.

He really didn't care.

He began to suck at one nipple, and sucked and sucked and sucked. It stiffened in his mouth, and the creature began to writhe sensually, and he realised that he was pleasing her. He sucked harder, and her whole body tensed, and then she sprayed into his mouth. The liquid that squirted out into his mouth tasted not of milk but of sex-juice, as if he were rolling his tongue over the wells of her pussy instead, as if he were sucking away at her clit and the flow had dripped down to his lips. This genital juice tasted also of something like, but not, burnt sugar. Burnt peppermint – everything tasted menthol, mint, like peppermint candy tablets that dissolve on the tongue, like wintergreen, spearmint...

He sucked the juices from each nipple in turn, one-two-three, drinking down this refreshing fluid that tasted of pussy. He wanted to drive his cock into her, soak it in her juices.

He continued to suckle but, even as he did so, shock hit his brain at last. Goddamn. It was too much of a cliché, myth that had been related for millennia by misogynists and feminists. He even remembered it from his undergraduate studies of ante-millennial literature (his dissertation had been pretentiously titled 'The

Sci-fi Cliché #10

1860s: The Industrial Evolution of Literature', and even now he winced at the memory). And there was that mnemonic device he'd used for his exams: *World of Women, World of Men: Sci-fi Cliché #10*. 'World of Women' said more about twentieth-century society than its corrollary. The misogynist take went like this: the females were neutered by their one-genderedness and male potency would set them free; would show them what they had always unknowingly craved – the supremacy of prick. And the feminist version had been utopian; the females had no need of men; they enclosed their own circles and their own needs, carnal or otherwise, yadda, yadda, yadda. In regard to the former, Sascha could even recall an ancient text of a film with the immortal Zsa Zsa: *The Queen of the Venusians*, or something similar. Even that had never rolled his socks up. He had stuck mainly with the eighteenth and nineteenth centuries. Aliens had always kind of creeped him out... previously.

This world felt like neither version, anyway. It was sufficient unto itself, and yet open to him as voyeur, open to him as partial, and perhaps even full, participant.

The alien was pressing his head down on her nipple again, quite forcefully, and he found he didn't *want* to participate. He wanted to observe nature in its original, untampered state. So he drew away from her insinuating embraces, his cock still thickened and stiff.

Two different females had approached, and were observing him attentively. These two were a little taller than the others, and Sascha figured that they were more mature. There was something else different about them other than their height, which he realised when they drew closer. On these two, their throats were covered with a layer of well-trimmed fur. One alien's fur choker was greyish, and that of the other female was bluer, bluer even than her otherwise bare skin. For some reason, this adornment aroused him even more; the fur seemed so sexual, so... provocative. Like private hair exposed, such as on humans: underneath the arms, between the legs. The creature whose tits he had sucked had seemed as giddy as a twenty-year-old, whereas these two seemed more reflective. Wiser. He grew a little nervous. All the females here were patently adults, but these two had a gravitas that made him think they might be the leaders. He tried to think of something responsible and logical to say in this case, but all he could find himself thinking about was their throat-fur, and what it would feel like to come all over it, in a fountain of semen. Oh, damn it. Had he no survival instinct at all? What about Severn? But all he could do now was remember the taste of that juice and stare at the fur round their vulnerable necks, as thin as human necks, as thin as his own. He thought of silver mink, silver furs, ice-queen furs. If he licked his own come out of that silky, smooth fur, it would taste like blue vanilla ice cream. Or maybe blueberry ice cream. Let me taste you, ice queens. Let me lick you. Let me come all over you.

The blue-furred female reached for the grey-furred one – hurriedly, nearly violently, and Sascha took yet another step back, this time completely out of the way. His mouth still tingled from the taste of alien tit-juice. But instead he watched as Blue spread Grey's thighs apart again, exposing all that luscious pink to his eyes. Grey was taller and presumably stronger, but still she submitted totally to Blue's caresses. Sascha swallowed hard, as his throat had suddenly gone dry. Damn it. It seemed like Blue was willing him to look at Grey's pussy. But instead he looked Blue in the eye, before lowering his gaze slowly to the fur ringing her throat. That soft, soft fur... He jerked his head up again. Yes, they were both staring at him, waiting for him to look down at that pink crotch. He did, and her pussy was wet and gleaming and slick. Then Grey put a hand down on herself and started to rub, started to grind her fingers hard against her stiff clit.

Oh, god. His cock was growing stiff, thickening again, but where else was he supposed to look? This was very perverse, too,

Sci-fi Cliché #10

watching this... beast pleasure herself with such abandon. Just look at that fur on her. Just look at that satiny, cool blue skin. Just look at that pink wet hole. He broke out in a cold sweat. He made himself look away but, wherever he looked, the blue creatures had started fucking, as if Grey's self-fingering had been a huge big signal for everyone to go at it as well, to go at it like fucking bonobo chimps, actually. There was abandon everywhere: grunting and groaning and the slurping sound of licking and fucking and fisting and deep-tongued kissing.

Sascha tore his eyes away at last. There was an erotic pull inside his gut, one that dragged way down to the pit of his stomach. His cock was tight, too thick. He no longer wanted to come on their throats; now he wanted to shove into one of their pink cunts: take them from behind and plunge his cock into the hot warmth, slick and oozing and wet for him; run his hand over their smooth blue asses, and just push and push and push until he came. There was all this female flesh. But he didn't feel right, somehow, touching it. It didn't feel right. Not at the moment. Maybe some other time. If they let him. But he could touch himself, and now his arousal had sweetened, and now it was tightening into something more painful, more desperate.

They were all fucking, all around him. All the blue aliens were screwing in that hot white sun, even screwing knee-deep in the river. He grabbed his cock, and his hand felt so good on himself, felt like a cool quick favour as he stroked himself more and more quickly, the sunlight hot on his neck, and as he watched Blue thrust one hand deep into the wide, candy-pink cunt, her blue fingers disappearing into that wet delicious hole, her thumb pressing down hard on the erect blue bead of the other female's clit. Then Grey's tits splashed out a glittering spray of blue liquid, three jets spurting out like miniature geysers, and then he winced with the sugary pain of the rush he felt all the way down the length of his cock.

He wanked and wanked and kept staring straight at the confectionery of Grey's splayed, open pussy, Blue's fingers fucking and Blue's thumb still just a-rubbing and a-rubbing, and he was still watching that same pink, that pink that had now turned nearly cherry with arousal and friction, when he groaned and tightened his fist and shot out his own liquid into the air. His knees buckled and he fell back, onto his ass, back on his hands. His whole body was shaking. His lips were dry. His throat was parched. His heart was beating like a fucking ancient metronome from before the 1860s Industrial Evolution, Revolution, whatever.

He hoped that water was safe, because he was going to go and take a drink from the river. And maybe take a bath, as well.

*

Her pod had crash-landed fifteen minutes ago.

Because impact had been violent, because impact had rent a huge great hole in the ship that let the air roar in, Severn had learned quickly that she could breathe the foreign atmosphere. Then she had stumbled out. Sascha's pod was nowhere in sight, and she thought she remembered that they had ejected at one and the same time, that she had caught a glimpse in the window-screen of another fireball hurtling towards this world.

It was quite possible that he had found himself on the other side of the planet, where it might be evening instead of early morning as it was here, or might not. She hadn't yet had a chance to work out the rotation pattern of the planet in regard to the dual suns, not in fifteen minutes, anyway. She wondered how he was coping. She wondered if there was life on this planet, and how he was coping with that, because Sascha could actually be a little alienphobic, if there was such a thing as a 'little' alienphobic.

It looked a lot like Earth, except for the two suns. The grass was bright green, the sky was blue and the bright daylight a warm,

Sci-fi Cliché #10

comforting yellow. She was standing on some form of a steppe, she reckoned, some sort of plateau. Except it had to be a very big plateau, maybe even a prairie, because it stretched out as far as the eye could see, the green grass rippling in the light wind. It was actually kind of pleasant, in a boring sort of way. There were no visible mountains or caverns or rivers to break up the view, though. She had once read that the naked human eye could see for seven miles, but she reckoned it was lot further than that when it came to big things like mountains. Severn always had her eye glued to a lens or a scope anyway, so she had never thought about it much.

Hell. The sunlight really was scorching. She was a little worried about sunburn or, worse, sunstroke, so she constructed a bandanna out of one of the torn parachutes. She had no food nor sustenance; she supposed she could eat the grass if it didn't poison her, but she was going to have to find some source of proper water soon. There were no rocks around that she could see, not even pebbles, so she broke off a long shard of her ship door and used it as a kind of marker, gouging a trail into the grass from time to time as she walked further away from the ship. Hansel and Gretel, eat your heart out.

As she walked along in the sticky but necessary lightweight spacesuit, it wasn't long before she began to be aware of two things. The first was that the endless lawn had a line drawn across it, though the line was becoming thicker and expanding as she progressed. The second thing she noticed was that there was a sound coming from up ahead as well, a sound that, as she continued to walk forward, intensified into what was undeniably music. It was spooky and high pitched, uncanny, but it was still music. There was more rhythm to it than the chaotic tune of wind, for example. It sounded a bit like vocal classical music. This meant either that there was organic life, or that organic life had once been here and had created a machine. Severn had been a spacer long enough to know that there was a difference between the two, and long enough to know that there were plenty of deserted, previously inhabited worlds sulking about in this quadrant.

So when the line finally revealed itself to be a huge but narrow chasm separating two stretches of the lawn, and when it became apparent that the music was emanating precisely from that huge, jagged hole, Severn began for the first time to get a little nervous. The thing was, she was also getting a little thirsty. So instead of slowing down, she speeded up.

Then she was standing at the lip of the cavern. Then she was staring down, down into this big crack of a canyon that wiggled its way endlessly to her left and endlessly to her right, made of chalk-like grey rock and dust. And then she was staring, open-mouthed in shock that her years as a spacer really shouldn't have permitted her to feel, at the valley below, a valley of grey rock and green grass and many, many green aliens walking around, too many to count, really. They were the ones who were singing, but this did not at first concern her. The first thing she thought actually was: water! There must be water somewhere. Life means water. Then she thought: perhaps they will kill me.

Of course, if she didn't approach them and approach them peacefully, she would die in a matter of days from lack of water. She vaguely wondered again how Sascha was faring, him and the fact that he had always had that problem with aliens. She really did need a drink.

And besides, they had already seen her.

She began to crawl down into the cavern. She got the chance to look more closely at them as they stared at her, still singing. She could now see that though their flesh was a pale, almost ghostly green, their lips and mouths were fringed with red, like bright exotic fish.

She was nearly upon them. Their raspberry-red mouths stirred something inside Severn; it was the blood-redness inside of their

Sci-fi Cliché #10

mouths in contrast to their stable, cool, melon-green. It was like all the carnality of their flesh was concentrated just inside the lips, indicating god knows what perverse pleasures, and the rest of their pale green bodies were controlled, even dispassionate. Yet that sharp, animal red – like raw meat, like a wound daubed with lipstick. She found herself watching their lips even when they stopped singing and stood staring at her: chill, dry-skinned, vaguely reptilian. She grew aware that she was looking for that glimpse of red again. She closed her eyes in shame. The image of the red stayed with her, a bright cloud of rouge in her mind. She started to tremble. She found herself wanting to pry their mouths open, to force her fingers in so that she could press them up against all the wet, shiny red.

It was the heat that made her think things like that. She needed a drink.

They were all male.

'Do you have any water?' she asked.

They started to sing again. She pointed to her mouth, miming for water.

One of the green men – fucking green men! she thought, like a old space movie – walked towards her. He was completely humanoid, and the odd glint in his eye reminded her of Naomi, her tomboy pilot colleague who had been as cocky as hell until her fighter had been blown out of the sky five years ago. Severn had no idea why she suddenly thought of Naomi. Maybe she was getting sunstroke after all. Those suns were hot. Severn pointed to her lips again. 'Water,' she repeated.

The alien that had walked up to her so boldly – she decided to call him Naomi – stood so close that she hoped he wasn't going to bite her. What was this, a medical examination? A new version of the old 'alien abduction' story? Jesus, how red was that mouth? The flesh was nearly scarlet; it looked almost sexual. Naomi's tongue, lips and mouth were such a darkened, ruby red that the shade was venous, like expensive claret wine. She needed a drink.

But of water, not wine.

Though wine would be okay, too.

In resignation, she pointed one final time to her mouth, and then pointed straight at Naomi. She didn't even say the word 'water' this time, but she certainly thought it.

Naomi was looking back at her. His alien face was strangely impassive. But surely they were mammals or reptilian or even amphibians of some sort. They needed water, just like she did.

Another alien was joining them. He was more slender than Naomi. It was inappropriate, but she found herself admiring his gait, the swing of his full, plump testicles – like two ripe, ripe pears, juicy and delicious and smooth in the throat. Jesus. Severn thought she might die of heat soon. She had to find some shade, if nothing else. But if she walked away, she might insult them, and then where would she be? Dead, or maybe captured...

The new alien had dropped to his knees in front of Naomi. He was a skinny, pretty young thing. He had opened his mouth.

Jesus. Was he actually going to do what she thought he was going to do?

Yes. And Naomi's cock was already hard as the grey rock she stood on, only with a smooth sheen to it, like a greased fruit. His attention had shifted from her; he was now groaning instead of singing, and thrusting his prick deep down Slim's throat.

Severn thought she might need to sit down. But she couldn't tear her eyes away from Naomi's melon-green prick, pushing back and forth in the slender alien's crimson mouth; it made her think that the mouths had evolved that way, sexual signifiers, like baboon asses, but then she was a rocket scientist, wasn't she, not a fucking evolutionary primatologist...

It was making her hot. She was *already* hot from the sun, and the last thing she needed was an onslaught of horniness. But that slick tight prick sliding into that red hole, with Slim starting to jerk off as well, his hand moving furiously over his own cock, and

Sci-fi Cliché #10

Naomi grunting with pleasure, screwing his eyes tight like any human guy getting sucked off – well, jeez, it was hot. It really was. She sank down on the slope of the cavern and watched the show.

By the time Naomi was shoving his cock repeatedly faster in a familiar rhythm, Severn had undone the zipper of her suit. By the time Slim had withdrawn his delicious mouth slowly from Naomi's thickened cock, Severn had two fingers up her cunt and was panting. And by the time Slim's strawberry-red tongue was licking its magic over Naomi's asshole and Naomi had his cock in his own hand, Severn had started masturbating in earnest. Oh jesus, it was a hell of a show. Naomi's sea-green body, tight and lean, was visibly trembling as Slim licked his asshole – slowly, so slowly. Severn's fingers were sticky in her cunt and on her clit. Even her own hand felt obscene. Good. God, her fingers felt good. She was really juiced up. She loved watching men have sex together, particularly alien men. She was heading straight for a fucking wicked climax. Hold on, folks. Those red lips, rouged up and plumped, kissing and stroking the tight green hole. She was so fucking wet. Her whole body was shaking. Her crotch was soaking. Her hand was drenched. Faster and faster. It felt so good. The taut red tongue, wiggling and wiggling. Oh, she couldn't look away now.

Naomi would probably come before she did, his body was already cramping, but just the sight of him made something in her coil tight, and she started stroking her clit with her middle finger until it all twisted into sweet and sour pleasure. And it was right then – smack in the middle of her orgasm – that Naomi's jism hit her in the face, right on the lips: his semen was silvery and clear, but it tasted like something much darker, like chocolate or violet or rich coffee. She kept her finger on her clit and licked her mouth, so sweet, so sweet and heavy and delicious. She swallowed, and it was like she was drinking a shot of fine brandy: warmth, all the way down.

The sun was still hot. She lay back and lazily watched as Naomi took his turn at pleasuring Slim with a blow job that would roll the socks off any of the guys *she* knew. Green, red, green, red – the colours blurred before her eyes as lips drew back and then advanced over cock. Green. Red. Green.

Jesus, it felt good here in the sun. Basking with her spacesuit rolled down to her hips. She became aware of the greenies singing again, and this time she found the melody relaxing, not eerie.

You know, it was just possible that her thirst had been quenched.

Several weeks later Severn hitched a ride with Slim over to the other side of the planet, the grey side, where the girls lived. That was when she hooked up with Sascha again. She was pleased to see that he was... thriving.

They compared notes for a good half hour or so over a glass of exotic peppermint wine that Sascha pressed upon her, giggling and blushing together until Sascha heaved himself up to his feet and rubbed his hands together gleefully.

'You know, Severn. I think I've been cured of my little alien-phobia problem.'

'That's good.'

'It certainly is. It makes me want to taste new fruits. You certainly gave a stirring description of your little green friends and I'd like to think I did the same with my new friends. Whaddya say we trade sides for a while?'

It sounded good to Severn. She was about to head toward the huge blue castle when she realised that she wanted to say something to Sascha. For a second she hesitated, unsure how to express it, and then remembered that he had studied ante-millennial literature and film. Who was the writer? Well, she couldn't remember the writer, but she could remember the character.

She smiled at Sascha and squeezed his hand good-bye. 'See you in a while,' she said. 'To paraphrase Candide, this is truly the best of both worlds.'

Yep.

Reds

Reds

I

You know where I met her? Guess. You're close. You're so close. Red-hot, in fact. Guess.

I met her on the bus one day; I was sitting behind her. You've been there, too. You've longed to caress her beautiful hair: the colour fills your eyes; it's all that you can see. You know that if you touch it, stroke it, it will leave a stain behind on your fingers: a stain the shade of rust that you can look at and smell and lick in private and thereby remember the girl who sat ahead of you on that bus. Yeah. You've been there, all right.

The shade is flame. Yet my fingers are cooled by her locks like I held them under a faucet that drips wine. That's the shade, too. Fire and liquid. Yin and bloody yang. We've got a nice balance going on, her and me.

Now she is my girlfriend. You're envious now, aren't you? Now I wake up with all that colour draped across my throat. I beg her not to bind it up at night: I enjoy the risk of it while we sleep, her back to me, my arms round her – strands splayed in thin, insect-frail threads across my nostrils, my open lips. I enjoy the risk that I could smother in it any night of any night. It would be a poetic, mythic way to go, like drinking hemlock, like choking on a single goat hair in my milk.

I could choke on thousands of red hairs. Every night, I could die in my sleep. Yet I wake up thankful in the mornings and I watch the sunlight on her head. Red, gold, red, orange, red, mustard, red and gold again.

I always wake up first.

Redheads go grey late in life; even octogenarians have bright threads left amongst the white. I think this makes them special, like they are still marked people, still carrying proof of their crowns of glory. My grandmother has red hair. I scan the heads of old men and women for traces of auburn; I imagine what they looked like young; I see what they look like even now. Like queens, kings, aliens. Redheads are always different.

Many redheads dye their hair. This is bawdy, exciting. Sometimes I want to push down the population of this city into a vat of henna and then raise them up again, gasping and shining. When my lover leaves the house, I walk around and collect the filaments of hair from pillows, from the sofa where she might have laid her head, from the cracks of the floorboards.

I find the threads, and then I braid them.

You've been there too. You know what I'm talking about.

My room is already light, but when my girl is inside its walls I roll up the old-fashioned shades and make it brighter. I don't want her hair dulled by darkness. I want it to glitter in my room like a port, not starboard, beacon. I imagine my fourth-floor apartment as a lighthouse, now that she's in it. If I dared to turn myself from the light and look out the window, I would see a pilgrimage of citizens, drawn from the bus stops, the food-stamp lines, abandoning their cars like in an apocalyptic Hollywood flick, all drawn towards the lighthouse, this gleaming place that houses the light that is my true love's hair.

At moments like these, the whole atmosphere changes. No longer a room, just a temple for her godhead. And this room is full of her hair. And if I close my eyes, a thousand scarlet cobwebs will grow across the room in the instant it takes me to lower my lids, and that veil will prevent me from raising them again. So all I have left will be the scent of it, the thread-thin strips of it, and the scent of her and her wetness, and my own hole wet and heavy as I fall more and more deeply into the dream of her hair. It will be everything feminine, wicked, beautiful and strong, and I will gladly be blinded by it. Yes. Gladly.

But if I keep my eyes wide as she stands there, she will already have stripped away her clothes. I will circle her and she will smile: this will make my heart go moist; will make my skin tense and prickle. Her hair will fall in fractals – to her knees, at least – wave upon perfect cosmic wave of auburn hair, rusty fjords and scarlet trigonometric arcs and blonde thinned liquids: these parabolas all echo back on themselves into merely my beautiful girl with her long red hair, as lovely as Botticelli's Venus, who stands not in froth but on the floor of my city apartment.

A beautiful girl with her long red hair.

That's the shade.

Let down your long red hair.

No less, no more.

She revels in my attention; there is no doubt. There is no doubt she knows that she holds me bewitched.

Come on, princess. Don't keep me waiting now, y'hear? Let down your hair. Let down your hair.

But my girl is not a cruel girl – no, she is generous to a fault – and so when she draws me towards her, grasps me by the nape of the neck, by my own short hair and slowly, slowly pulls me tight into her until my nose and tongue and eyes and ears – all the most important parts of my head save the one concentrated in the small space of my skull – are up against the warm richness of her long hair, I see the gold-red wires sway like curtains, and then I close my eyes and it is like my smother-dream, after all. The rustle as she shakes her locks, the light rub and release of each individual fibril against my smooth cheeks. It's a lot, too much, and that is why I have to close my eyes, to imagine the colour so as not to truly see it. It's less intense that way.

Soft, soft on my face. I struggle to my knees, throw my arms round her calves, lost in the waterfall of her hair. I am no child seeking solace, but a pilgrim like all others. I want not comfort but to pay homage.

Stand up, she says.

(You wish you were here with me, don't you?)

My eyes are still closed. I cannot open them to look at the colour yet. That would be. Too much.

We are face to naked face, and then she steps back, and this motion does startle me into opening my eyes, and it's like I jacked a whole hit straight into my veins; it's the red after the B&W; it's the swirl and glide of her neck as she leans her head way, way back and slowly shakes out her hair.

Out in public I see the shade quickly, the auburn flicker amongst dull browns and predictable blondes. Most 'red' hair is not truly red – it's a burnished brown, a burnt orange. I'm not attracted by the degree of intensity or genuineness of the redness. I see the worth in the sun-bleached henna highlights of dark black hair as much as I do a blatantly dyed punkette lipstick-red. It's the nuances that get to me. It all gets to me. It's no coincidence: red flag to the bull, stop-signs, fire engines. Even the ink of my favourite ballpoint pen. (It's always a red-letter day for me.)

I imagine her twisting it into a braid and dangling it out the window: one floor down, two floors down, three floors down, all the way down to the asphalt below.

You would be there at the bottom. You would be first in line, sniffing like a dog for it, standing there waiting, salivating for a taste, the red lure swinging back and forth, back and forth... Others might crawl towards her despite their reluctance, but you would have no shame at all; no reason to hide your eagerness.

You're just like me. I used to watch 'I Love Lucy' just to feel my groin tighten. And that was in black and white. Just possibility. You're like me.

She lets me touch it. My palms flat against the undulating, fragile silkstrands. These same hands of mine shake as I walk half a circumference and no longer see her face. Only a river of red. My eyes blur with liquid: the tint strengthens from hair-red to the most familiar shade of all. Let's say the word: blood. Let's not be afraid of a single syllable. I'm sure that's what you think it's all about, and I'm not convinced it isn't.

Oh jesus: that warm, slightly damp softness against my fingertips. Not cool at all now, her hair. Warmed up. Like an animal. Like it's alive after all. My sight now veiled and the red river explodes – a flood – and it is only hair-red again, not wound-red. But the twin drops that roll out from each duct – well, I know that if I were to see these teardrops that they would be as red as the vein, two lurid pearls. I am in the presence of a miracle, so of course things like this happen: Vatican statues secrete real tears to great applause; women weep blood. My tears fall to the floor unobserved.

I cannot see her face any more than I can see my own. But I can tell that she is panting. I can tell that she is ready for it.

Three even divisions, each as thick and tensile as my own arm. Right length into middle, cross over the left, right into middle, cross over left. Three sections, two movements, one product. A fucking trinity all on its own. And you would suggest this is not a holy act?

The plait reaches down past the back of her knees.

I am pulled just as you are. I am pulled and not released. She lets down her hair. She lets down her long red hair. She puts her hand down on her cunt.

Her hair is rubbed between my legs like a dampened rope; her braid sends shivers through me, makes my whole flesh tremble, as back and forth the braid goes along my pussy; I'm riding it, grinding down on it. It's so intimate, shoving myself down on the hard braid of her hair.

Don't you think so? Don't you think so? Don't you wish it was you, up here in the sunlit room with my bright shining girl, your juice on her hair and not mine? Instead there you are, four floors below, reckless for just a taste of what I've got. She pulls her hair, I come. That's how it is.

And you then, four floors below with the rest of the city desperadoes, feeling the pull too, feeling the ache of the plait, always just inches out of reach. I know precisely how you feel it. I know you feel it.

II

Poison was a funny thing, particularly a poisoning by hair. It seemed at first thought impossible. If she had a second choice, it would be something a bit softer like ether or opiates. Still, hair's what the doctor ordered and hair it would have to be.

It had been her decision, anyway. He was trouble, sitting outside the door screaming that she didn't give a damn or even know his name. And there she sat working so hard inside the fourth-floor apartment, spinning her hair into coils of red gold for the man on the other side of the door.

Her hands whirled round each other, round and round they went, spooling up the copper flax into a bundle; snap went the scissors; a heap of spun gold fell to the floor. It was all for the man who waited outside the door. Eventually, she would always let him in.

Soon she would be bald.

He exacted his price: she spun him gold every week, red gold, and in return he gave her hard cold green cash. Metal was prettier, absolutely, and it glittered just so, but it was so difficult to explain at the pawnshops, and the little man outside the door did all of that business for her. He gave her cold green cash. She gave him hot crimson gold. He gave her money. She gave him a little bit of honey. That's how the transaction went. Green for red and red for green. As predictable as a traffic light. If one stares at red for quite a while and then at a blank white wall, it turns green. And green turns red. That's how the transaction worked, between the little man and her.

She didn't even know his name. True. He wanted her to ask, she could tell, when his breath was in her ear and his fingers were inside her, her hips thrust upwards, but she never did ask.

She saw him on the fourth floor on days when her lover was absent. She thought that her lover, Laura, knew that he came; knew that her hair was thinner on those days that he visited, but Laura never said a word and neither did she.

The man paid for his gold and he got it. Her gold was like the sun – like blood mixed with honey, like wine mixed with urine, like sour cranberry juice blended into pine sap. It was not all sweet, as you can see. Her love could be bitter.

She was strangely addicted to him. His predatory nature drew her closer; she sometimes looked forward to those afternoons on which he appeared: he was the bad and bitter parts of her and sometimes she needed that kind of sleaze, needed to feel the dirt on her and the dirt on him, the hard exchange of currency and half-orgasms, the inadequate fumblings, his tongue filthy in her mouth and her sucking it in shame, secretly enjoying it. Her breath quickening and the shame of him hearing it go ragged, the shame of him knowing that sometimes she looked forward to those afternoons. Oh, the shame.

Still, he had to go. She suggested it one morning herself, and Laura seemed to have no problem with the idea.

You see, it was hard to be in thrall to a person. The pimp dynamic is inherently skewed and she was fighting back for her cut of all that cash. She had grown tired of being his cow, milking out her hair for him, winding it up on wooden spools of coiled red gold. It stimulated but exhausted a girl, this type of nursing, this type of parasitism.

So it was her idea, but it was Laura who put the germ of the idea in her head. They were lying in bed together, radiantly happy, satiated, and she had asked Laura, 'If you were to poison someone, how would you go about it?' And Laura had said that the best way to die would be by hair alone – this was a predictable response on the part of Laura, so no points at all for originality.

But it had got her thinking. She had once read of a Mafia target poisoned by eating ground-up glass. If glass could hurt, then she reckoned surely hair could too, and what more befitting way for him to perish, the little man who held her captive by her dependence on his cash and on his cock. She longed to leave the room in the afternoons, to become a pirate and sail the seas, a cowboy, an aviatrix, to be free of him, but he held her there, and no one would understand why that was a crime too, one just as bad as a poisoning might be.

And it was those bad parts of her, too, that came out when he was there. The parts that made her feel tarnished and animalistic – like she had *fur* instead of hair – and not at all like the goddess she felt like when she was with her lover Laura. The bits where she licked his skin from ear to toe and still wanted more, wanted to ingest him. She could poison away those parts of her too. Hair poison. He would ingest her. It was quite suitable for the parasite he was, when all was said and done.

So she planned her escape carefully. She would feed the same substance to him, on each visit, creating a hairball in his stomach. Then one fine day she would lure him in; would sell him more hair than ever he had bought before, and then the poisoning would be complete and he could no longer nurse her strength away from her like the Delilah he was. It would weigh him down, turn to red gold in his stomach. And everyone knew that gold was poisonous.

And so this is exactly what she did. Each time he came to her in the afternoon light, each time she clung to him still wet with her own sweat, she fed him dainties and small candies, iced with black-eyed susans and suns and marzipan tangerines, everything bright and sparkling as her own head. But into this confectionery she mixed chopped-up bits of her hair. Laura often left small braids of it around the apartment and these she found and pocketed and then hashed up later with a great glittering steel knife and baked into the tiny cupcakes and petit fours that she would offer the man on his ever-increasing afternoon visits.

At last the day arrived. Even as he entered the apartment, she hid a secret smile, thinking of those parts of her already festering inside his stomach. Yet this day his charm was complete. She had never felt her heart beat quite so quickly in his presence as it did this afternoon. He seemed more powerful than ever before and she sucked his cock with an eagerness that she had avoided previously: every move seemed poignant, since it was last. He squeezed the points of her nipples until they felt like they were being burnt; he slid his tongue around the nape of her neck and she trembled with lust. She still didn't know his name and she didn't even want to guess. She was in thrall to him, but of course she had her secrets too. Still, when she smelled his breath she was wet for him and worked his cock slowly into her hole, savouring every slow angry inch. They fucked well together – not a graceful dance at all, but a cumbersome, clumsy slither of a fuck and she much preferred that to elegance.

He took all her hair that day. He left her as bald as a onion. When they had finished fucking and her heart was still pounding from the orgasm she'd squeezed out despite herself, the grimy climax her body and his fingers had betrayed her by, she saw all over the room the hundreds of spools of delicate cord wound like spiders' webs, the ribbons of red ingot that now were his alone.

She recovered her breath and stared him out in the afternoon light of the room. He looked impervious and smug. She waited for him to expire to the poison she had concocted, because she knew exactly the price she had paid for it.

III

Gavin watched them enter the building, both Laura and Eve. He drank his takeaway latte too quickly and then crumpled up the disposable cup, as if he could relieve a little passion on the soggy cardboard itself. Once upon a time he had had a thing going on with Eve, quite a sweet deal in fact. But no longer.

Eve the redhead was the most beautiful girl – with the most lovely hair – on earth. Sometimes these days he passed them both in the street. Eve would ignore him, but he could sense her girlfriend, Laura, cute enough in her own way, sniffing him and his motives out. She might smirk at him; once she even put a proprietorial hand up to fondle those soft auburn tresses.

If only she knew.

Gavin, in fact, once had had bundles of Eve's hair piled up in his student-style attic apartment, because of course he and Eve had this thing going then, but like all truly sweet things it came to an untimely end. Just as well. He had been anxious every time he came round to her place, which actually was her girlfriend's place, knowing that Laura could walk in at any moment. He truly would get nervous pains in his gut just going over there, and no one was worth that kind of stress, really. No one. The stomach aches got worse and worse. Even his doctor had told him to give the girl up. It's not a happy position, being the Other Man. Or, in this case, the only man.

They were a lovely couple, really. It killed Gavin to admit it, but it was so obvious from where he now stood, half hidden near some trees outside Laura's apartment building. They were one hot item. Still, Gavin had a secret to which even Eve was not privy, and it was this: Laura had known very well what was going on with him and Eve on those afternoons. Once Gavin saw her crying in the park on his way over to the apartment. But Laura was so smitten – and Gavin was too; he wasn't excusing himself from the whole messy equation – that Laura let them get away with it. Gavin did feel guilty, but he was so hung up on Eve at the time that he hadn't wanted to spoil it.

gavin holds a doll – it catches the sunlight filtered through the trees as he tips it back and forth – it fits entirely in his left hand: if he closes his fingers round it, the little red doll will vanish – gavin makes it disappear this way, but it's burning like a coal now and so are the memories – he and eve always had sex quickly and always the presence of her gorgeous, freakish hair was there like a third person in the room – she used to make him so hard – she'd pile it up on top of her head, heaps of lush curls – he would kiss her, his hand too quick to her crotch, his fingers too quick to rub the hem of her skirt and his cock fully hard and yes, too quick – all he wanted to do was cram it into her – his fingers straining to rip apart her skirt – their faces touching – already caught in the red mess of her hair, the smell of it fecund and ripe, then he would push his cock up inside her, then he would be ready, his prick stiffening tight & hot –
　the little red doll of hair, like a live coal in his palm

Gavin was a passionate man at heart. He hadn't always been, particularly not when he was seeing Eve on the sly. Eve once called him the least romantic fuck on the planet. Probably because he slipped her the odd twenty or fifty even though he knew it made her feel like shit, because he also knew the two of them, Eve and Laura, could really use the money. A more broke pair of dykes he'd never met. Even though it stung like hell to be doing a favour for

Laura, he'd been generous with his cash and unappreciated.

And then there was the wigmaker. That's where it had gone wrong. Yeah – the wigmaker who said he'd pay a proper tidy sum for authentic red hair and it all went downhill from there. Usually, the wigmaker used hair from Asia – imported dark hair subsequently bleached and dyed red. It was a nasty business, really, the hair business – built on broken dreams and poor desperate women. Gavin should have never got mixed up in all that, but at the time he'd thought that he was doing Eve a favour. Let's face it, she was no Ms Donald Trump. And he'd do anything for Eve, but this time he'd really stuck his foot in it, really fucked up. Hair extensions for other rich white women – no, Eve was worth much more than that. Every woman was worth much more than that.

the red doll in his right hand is making his palm sweat – this doll he calls laura – little manikin laura is woven carefully from leftover strands gavin has plucked up from around his attic – the filaments glowing thin and scarlet and violent in the dark – they were easy to find, those hairs – he has tied them up into laura the homunculus and then a little eve, using the hair itself as binding – a doll in each hand, he squeezes tight but they don't feel as real as the two women who have just entered the apartment building – gavin in the green trees grips his dolls and reflects on eve's now-smooth skull – his breath is coming fast –

well neither of these dolls has hair atop their heads at all

Gavin could see it in her eyes even then that she wanted to break it off, as soon as he brought up the wigmaker in conversation for the first time, and he was still so hungry for her at that point that he couldn't deal. He really couldn't. He could tell the split-up was coming, but even so he'd stayed around for it. She was so lovely. Her body was as pale as milk and she was covered head to toe with light freckles, like constellations poured over her entire flesh. He once tried to kiss every freckle on her body, but only made it as far down as her neck before his lips felt bruised. Her pussy was soft and snug and juicy, her pubic hair the auburn fuzz of a sunbaked Florida peach. She was a real redhead, for sure. Sometimes he would just lay his head in her lap and rub up against the pelt of her hair, the supple yet stiff strands brushing his cheeks, his nose still full of the scent of pussy sap, her sweet cunt still smeared over his face, her loosened braid tickling his neck and bare shoulders. Gavin didn't wonder that her girlfriend ached with love for her, because the truth was he did too. The truth even was: he still did.

gavin slackens his fingers on the laura doll and places it in his left hand with the eve – he digs in his pocket for that old camel lighter for which he'd smoked far too many cigarettes to earn by coupon – there it was, now his fingers found it – they were up there in the apartment by now, up in the apartment he knew only too well, kissing no doubt touching no doubt fucking – he'd seen the love still there in laura's eyes even when they'd walked past – gavin grips the silver-plated lighter, thumb to flint and freezes – the wind rustles through the tree leaves – light would be streaming through the apartment by this time in the afternoon – gavin knows the pace of every minute of the afternoon – every hesitation and fumbling rush – gavin begins to weep now, his thumb trembling on the rough flint wheel –

he has no strength to summon a spark

Eve had paid him off, finally. It's not pretty being dumped. Gavin had to come to terms with the fact that he had only ever meant funding to the girl. Red-haired Eve had never loved him, not the way he'd felt for her. She never even liked to use his name. That hurt. That was one of those things that used to cause his gut to ache. One day he had come over – ready for an afternoon of heat and light and sweat. That was the first time he and Laura had met face to face. That hadn't been pretty, either. They'd had words. But the gist of it all, after the recriminations had been uttered, was that

Laura had stepped back and let him climb into the elevator. She had said: go on, Gavin, if you're what she wants, then I can't deny her even you, even you, you fucked-up, short-assed little grunge boy. Gavin had been stung, but he'd still stepped into the elevator, feeling the thrill of triumph. Laura had sold her claim. He had bought it. Going, going, gone.

Eve had been waiting in the room. Sunlight had filled the space and made her hair glitter; made it shine like Liberace. Nothing could ever shine like Eve's hair had done that day. Eve's hair – not a strand of it on her head, either. All around the room were piles of it; she'd cut and shaved and depilated and there it was.

'Take it.' Eve's eyes and voice had been cold. 'Take it, and get out.'

Well, what would you do? Like Laura, Gavin had loved Eve even then, but he was no fool. He had a student loan to pay off and we're talking a lot of money here. He'd piled his arms with the riches, red flax, spun hair sugar spilling from his burdened biceps, and he'd hit the road. On the way out on the ground floor, he'd run into Laura. He'd been nasty, said something about the fact that she'd been bartering soiled goods, that she and Eve had sold each other out. Laura had given him a blank, blank look and he'd hurried out with his ill-gotten treasure.

But she'd stuck by Eve and Eve by her, after all that. That was really something. Gavin closed his eyes and remembered Eve's long braid snaking its way down over her shoulderbones as he lay on his back and she fucked him; remembered the red-rush-roar of blood in his ears; the jerk of her hips, her tight thick cunt, candy-sweet, the clarity of his feelings for her, or so it had seemed back then: her cunt, his cock, her hair; the three of them in that room flooded with sunlight, so that every dust particle was visible, every thousandth hair –

gavin's thumb goes click and the flame is lit – flame on the first doll, flame on the second – he presses their heads together, the hair is spitting fire and gold cinders – they both grow manes of red-gold blaze – he looks at them –

his hands are tender

In the fourth-floor room, the two women kiss. Locks of fire-hot hair emerge from the paler girl's head, tumbling down, so fast they grow, down to her knees – the other girl puts a hand to touch them, she is frightened of being burned twice, but not so scared she won't allow herself to touch. The kiss holds them, tentative, their own arms hold them, the hair holds them. It winds round them, binds them tight, so sealed.

Sister Six

Sister Six

In the beginning there were twelve. Twelve like the twelve apostles, twelve like the twelve months of the year, twelve like the twelve commandments. Sorry. That's wrong. But you get the picture.

They ranged from nineteen up to a certain age (okay then, 30) and they were all single births. Think of the poor mother. If there'd been a couple of twin pairs or triplets in the mix, she could have retired a little earlier. But instead she popped one out like clockwork every year; yes, exactly, like the twelve hours of the day; yes, exactly, hard work like the twelve days it took God to create Heaven and Earth. No. But you get the picture.

Their mother was a glamorous woman. In fact, she looked exactly like the Countess in *The Sound of Music*, the beautiful nasty one that Von Trapp dumps for goody-good Maria. As a matter of fact, their mother shared the Countess's views on bringing up children: 'A delightful little thing called boarding school,' she said to their father, who was completely smitten with his wife and would never dream of running off with some nun. Besides, husband and wife had had nearly twice as many kids as the Von Trapps. So there.

So, off the girls all went to boarding school followed by communal living at a rather strict student dormitory (associated with a university from which none of them, so far, had graduated) and by the time the last of them had become a young woman, they were beauties famed the world over. They always made the top twelve of *People* magazine's 50 Most Beautiful People list, though the positioning varied. Sometimes skinny was in, and that would be frail ethereal Ursula at No. 1; sometimes it was juicy Diana Dors-alike Magden. Lovelies Cecily, Ellen, Erica, Erin, Polly, Allison, Sara, Victoria, Dorothy and Mona had all had their moments in the sun as well.

It's hard to concentrate on twelve separate viewpoints, so from hereon we're sticking with Polly, number six of twelve, 25 years old. She had short brown hair which was fairly tomboyish but the gossip rags just loved it, and her, and always insisted on calling it 'gamine'.

Now, here's the scoop: the girls had taken to sneaking out of the dorms every night and cabbing it to London superclubs, but by 2003 the superclub had had its day, even in London, thank god, so instead of wearing out their shoes dancing every night, the sisters began hanging around intimate jazz venues, smoking etc. Hell, it was just a lot less aggro than a club and you didn't have to worry the whole time about dodgy E, either. Although it has to be said that the switch to low-gear entertainment was initiated by the three oldest – Mona, Dorothy and Victoria – and that's what happens to every urban club kid when they hit their late twenties. Still, follow the leader, all the girls were chilling out at gastropubs and Hoxton cinemacafés these days, chatting to the regular scene werewolves and vampires and witches, getting so drunk on Cosmopolitans that when they stumbled home at night the streetlights and the trees would blend together until it looked like the branches were strung with shimmering lights, gold and silver and bronze, that's what good old alcoholic double vision will do to a girl.

Pretty Polly, who'd had one Margarita early in the evening and stopped there, dragged her feet behind her eleven sisters, who had their arms around each other and were singing 'I Should Be So

Sister Six

Lucky' off-key for the fourth time, generally intimidating all passers-by and commenting loudly on the packet of any male under seventy.

It was all starting to feel stale these days for Polly, and just too fucking predictable. Sow your wild oats, yeah yeah yeah; a Gap year and then college; meet a nice boy in your early thirties and settle down. That's all twelve dancing princesses have waiting for them in life, let's face it. To add insult to injury, they don't even get to choose; they have to be chosen by a prince who has flattered up their dad; chosen, like being picked out of a Miss Universe line-up. Polly wanted out. But how?

She kicked a Coke can morosely up Upper Street, still following her sisters. The area was affluent and it was unusual for there to be any trash on the pavement at all. The streetcleaners were well and frequently paid.

She nearly knocked over another morose young person, a handsome dark-haired man with a chiselled jaw and a cleft in his chin. She recognised him from last year's 50 Most Beautiful list. He had been No. 34. She had been No. 7, an unfortunate rash on her left cheek.

'I know you!' she exclaimed suddenly, as vulnerable to celebrity-worship as the rest of us, 'you're Prince Charming! You're engaged to Sleepy!' The wedding was next week. She had absolutely no clue why he looked so glum. She hoped he realised that she had meant the Sleeping Princess, not the dwarf. (Bashful, not Sleepy, was definitely the best of *that* lot.)

He gave her a small smile, and even that only eventually. 'Yes. That was my own fault. I should never have kissed her. How was I to know? All of a sudden, the banns were announced and the date was set. She doesn't even like me,' he confided, 'she just wants my money and the title. She thinks I'm boring. I overheard her telling her friend Stacia on the phone the other night. I'm trapped in a happy ending.'

He stared with quiet anger at the Frappucino advertisement in the window of Starbucks.

Polly ran her fingers through her charmingly short haircut. She had a feeling it was sticking straight up. She guessed it probably looked all right. It always did. She bent in and put her nose in his hair, dark like her own.

It smelled nice. Freshly shampooed. She kissed his earlobe and watched him shiver and then grin. He looked at her intently. His eyes were quite exciting, she suddenly observed. Now at last she recalled them from the Most Eligible Bachelors special on TV last week. Soulful, even. He pulled her to him. She felt his cock, hard against her groin. He felt like a man, not a fairy-tale cipher.

'Okay, come with me if you want to,' he said firmly, and she agreed just as firmly and took the hand he was offering. He led her down to his car, parked in the shadows of Islington Green. For all its wealth, the Council still hadn't got the streetlamps working again. His car wasn't as expensive as she had expected. It was dark where he'd chosen to park. The tree-sieved moonlight dappled the leather car seats. They closed the doors. People walked past. Nobody could see in. She sucked his cock and it was tangy, clean, meaty in her mouth. It tasted very good. She liked the fact that she had made him so stiff. And he sat beside her on the back seat and sealed his fingers inside her panties, touching her until she was warm and sticky on them, rubbing his thumb against her clit until she began to shake, and moan, and come, twisting her hips against the strength of his wrist.

If someone walked by, they would only see them sat demurely side by side and not know that his fingers were still tight down her pants, his fingertips still wet, just brushing the edges of her hole, his wrist warm from the friction. But the steamed-up windows might be a bit of a giveaway.

Sister Six

'What now?' he said. He looked at her in the moonlight and she saw that he looked scared. He wasn't trying to be cool. She felt scared too.

'We'll start with happily ever after and move on to once upon a time, then go on from there,' she told him, 'now we change the story.'

Serpents, Corn and Honey

Serpents, Corn and Honey

The Mixtec Period / Monte Albán, Mexico, 1071 AD

So Lady 4 Alligator left the temple only moments before the royal banquet.

She walked along the wide steps that led down from the shrine, down to the main path that headed towards the observatory. She had been warned to be on time, so if she ended up arriving late, it would be entirely her own fault.

'You're going the wrong way,' her brother 13 Vulture informed her as he dashed past in the opposite direction, his tunic blown up by his very speed. 4 Alligator didn't respond, but on the other hand, he wasn't exactly waiting for a response, either. She put her hand to her own tunic. It was woven in contrasting blocks of black and white, the traditional priest's robe, everything perfect except for the one that wore it. She felt alien in it suddenly, like she was wearing another human's skin over her flesh, and she thought briefly of 13 Vulture in the flayed skin he had worn for the spring ceremony last year, and she blinked.

Then she stopped, straight in her tracks. She closed her eyes. All around her, she could feel a breeze as people rushed in the opposite direction. She stretched both hands out, and hit someone moving by on her right, and was cursed for it – quietly, though, because she was a priest. Still, she had a sphere around her which meant that people gave way. Because of the black-and-white tunic, of course. She kept her eyes closed and imagined someone looking down from the temple pyramid, seeing her standing there on the lime-green stone while others rushed past, a stone in a stream, an obstruction. She flashed her eyes open again in the bright light – yes, they would be able to see her leaving. It was better to turn around and go back, and make up some excuse as to why she had stolen away in the first place. Reluctantly, she did so.

Lady 4 Alligator should have worn something else for her first major banquet, oh yes. She had a garment at home that was painted with the Jaguar. This god, who had the audacity to swallow the sun, had always been her favourite. How could you not admire such bravery?

She walked upwards on the broad steps again. Now she had joined the quiet crowd, like a fish, but the stream had slowed in reverence as it flowed up the pyramid and closer to glory and, though the steps were so huge, nearly plateaus, they were packed and movement was slow. Still, people moved aside for Lady 4 Alligator. It was an unusually dry and sunny afternoon. As black and reflective as the obsidian eyes that winked out from the geometrically carved wall depictions of the god Qchi 9 Wind, her hair shimmered in the gold beams of the day. She shone. She knew it. She shone with her status. But take off the tunic and she was only a woman of twenty-one summers. How would she be seen throughout the ceremony? She worried she might vomit.

'Four Alligator!' A voice was calling from up above. Yes, of course, 13 Vulture again, with some other priests. Well, she'd get there eventually. The steps were too congested. It was becoming difficult to walk. She took a few more paces, and then the crowd itself came to a halt, and not even the privilege of priesthood could move it. In the pause, and while people tried not to push

Serpents, Corn and Honey

against her, 4 Alligator took a look around – there, the frieze with the nude male dancers. The Dancers had been here for a very long time, it was said, left behind by the Old Ones. The faces of these dancing figures were bald and blank. Their mouths were pursed; their noses thick. 4 Alligator noticed these things with a quiet concentration that meant that she did not have to think about the banquet or the ceremony. Yes, think about set things instead, things that have been here forever, stone things, astronomy, not squirming live things.

Lady 4 Alligator had no objection to sacrifice – though of course there were those who did object. She had sacrificed before, anyway, and her hand had held the red fruit of a heart, still pulsing, and she had felt only deliverance, and had known that the god Saqui 7 Earthquake had been pleased with the gift. No, Lady 4 Alligator was afraid of the attention itself, that her hands would slip with the knife, that she would drink from the wrong painted cup during the preceding banquet, that she would laugh if someone read from the incorrect codex if called up to recite. And today was not just any sacrifice: it was her first post-banquet ceremony as Oracular Priest. Ever. And even though her brothers had told her that everyone gets nervous, she couldn't imagine that they had ever been as nervous as she was now. Oh, no. It was not likely.

The crowd moved again, and Lady 4 Alligator went ever upwards on the steps that led to the greatest pyramid in the city, and left the Dancers behind her, and passed through the huge trunks of pillars that bordered the wide steps – which was humorous, in a way, for the rest of Monte Albán had no trees at all. And that was better. Trees lived. No trees. Stone trunks of pillars instead. Obsidian eyes, bare stone trees, the glitter of gold pendants that hung on the walls instead of sunlight, the green of the stone pavement instead of grass. Everything frozen. Good. Nothing would move, and she would never have to perform after the banquet, and she would not shame her family by throwing up all over Lord 7 Death, the kindly middle-aged priest who would be sitting by tradition on her left.

'Hurry, Four Alligator!' her brother shouted again, overeager. Now that was just plain embarrassing, oh yes. He needed to keep his mouth shut. Now all those around her would know that she was late, and unprepared, and of course they now would be watching her more closely during the ceremony, waiting for her to falter, waiting for her eventual failure.

Now at last she was nearing the top, and there were several tall men in front of her, and 4 Alligator experienced a welcome anonymity. 13 Vulture would not be able to see her and shout out to her. Well, she would join him soon enough. To her left, she saw the axes of the steps run off down a wide stretch, and she remembered that that was where the sacrifices were kept. There were two special ones reserved for her, she had been told, though she hadn't been informed as to what made them so distinct.

Last year she had seen a beautifully staged ceremony – a young man, taking each step of a pyramid slowly, breaking a flute as he reached each new level. And all around him had been beautiful girls who had cried as he ascended, had cried as if their hearts would break. Afterwards, he had been carried down, tenderly. It had been the most affecting of sacrifices.

She was level with the other priests now. But she faced their backs: they were looking at some unseen thing that had caught their interest. The way everyone here would be looking at her, after the banquet, when it was her turn for attention. 4 Alligator took a deep breath, like she was diving under water, and then she span round and pushed through some people behind her and darted unseen to the left, where the sacrifices were kept, and ran swiftly across the empty space. She moved behind a pillar so that she was hidden and when she peered out she saw that she was not missed at all; that the crowd was oblivious; that even her brother and the other priests still had their backs turned and their attention elsewhere. It was as good a place as any to submerge oneself and think.

Serpents, Corn and Honey

She slipped inside the corridor itself, and suddenly everything was very cool, and very dark.

Most of the sacrifices had been taken up already, though there were some here that still called out in hope to Lady 4 Alligator. She spoke gently to them, and walked on. There was fright, but she had been taught to be tender to those to be given to the gods, for the sacrifice and tribute came from them and not from her. She was only the umbilical cord.

It was difficult to make out the carvings of green serpentine, since it was so shadowy, but the corridor was a beautiful place even in its duskiness; there were coral mosaics and mirrors of obsidian fixed to the walls, and paintings littered with bar-and-dot mathematics that she could not read in the darkness, even if she squinted. There were also piles of fresh flowers here, though such blooms were heaped higher outside, of course, decorating the banquet and sacrifice areas. She could not make out what types of flowers they were, however. She just smelled a sweetness amongst the damp.

No, there was scarcely any light in here at all, and there was an area up ahead where there was so much screaming that Lady 4 Alligator felt ashamed on behalf of the noisemakers. As she drew closer, she heard that the sounds had the pattern of an unfamiliar language, and this explained the fuss. Foreigners always took it harder, lacking belief and therefore respect for the gods.

Having thought that, she had never heard such a squawk. She moved closer, fully aware at some level that this was all still a distraction, and that soon enough she would have to emerge into heat and light and duty. The noise suddenly bothered her. 'Shut up,' she hissed loudly, and then dug her nails into her palms, ashamed at having lost control. The noise was worse, horrible unintelligible animal sounds, and Lady 4 Alligator shrieked again for quiet. This time, the sounds stopped for a moment, and then they started up again even louder. Lady 4

Alligator turned into the alcove area, fumbled beneath her tunic and then in a pouch until she found her flint, and sparked a fire up on the torch that was fastened to the stone wall, then went round and lit three more, and only then did she turn around to see who was bound there.

There were naked two women, probably of her own age, but it was difficult to tell, since one had hair which was prematurely whitened. They were both blind. They were knotted tightly with rope, though not gagged; Lady 4 Alligator imagined this was because they had threatened to bite. Sometimes, the binders just gave up if they couldn't get the gags in place, and Lady 4 Alligator didn't blame them.

It was odd, though, because as she moved round them to get a better look at the rebels, their eyes followed her as if they could in fact see; though her grandfather, who lost his sight in later years, had also been able to do this by sound alone.

The white-haired one, who looked younger, began to weep, and then the older of the two women said to Lady 4 Alligator, in quite a terrible accent, 'Please.' The hair of the other woman glowed in contrast to the mosaic tiles of coral, amber and turquoise that lined the walls, images of eagles and antelope and maize and stars and bees and jaguars and rain and grasses. Yet despite the ornate surroundings, there was that same damp smell throughout the entire sacrifice corridor, like a room after a storm.

Lady 4 Alligator thrust a hand toward them, silently, and watched the older woman flinch. She was not blind, or not entirely blind. Curious. And perhaps the white-haired one was not entirely blind, either, though it was difficult to tell since she still hung her head and wept. The older one's eyes were the same colour as blue-green jade, or maybe an evening sky, but after the rain and not before it. Lady 4 Alligator had never before seen such a shade in someone's eyes who was not already sightless. Perhaps it was even these two who were destined to be her own 'special' sacrifices. She was intrigued, despite herself.

'Can you understand me?' She spoke slowly and carefully. Further along the corridor, she could hear the faint soft cries of future sacrifices in other alcoves.

'Yes,' answered the woman. She had a strange and croaking inflection, and Lady 4 Alligator saw how pale both their skins were, like that of someone very ill. Yet the two of them appeared healthy enough despite their pallor – well muscled and firm.

The first toast would be being orated by now, Lady 4 Alligator realised suddenly, and 13 Vulture would be wondering where she was, perhaps even panicking. She could stay a while longer, though, because there were at least ten books to be read out loud and enacted with due pageantry. As she was presiding over the sacrifice itself, she was for once exempt from the banquet theatricalities. There would be food too – roasted jackrabbit, antelope cooked with chillies, spicy cocoa, maize soaked in ash and lime and then ground and baked into tortillas, ones filled with lima beans and seeds. All of this eating would also take time.

'What are your names? Where do you come from? Why do you look so peculiar?' she asked curiously. The pale-haired woman raised her head up from her weeping at last and stared at Lady 4 Alligator with the same weird, unblind blue eyes. But this time Lady 4 Alligator seemed to have spoken too quickly for comprehension, because they conferred together in their rough tongue, and then it was the younger one who answered this time.

She spoke hesitatingly, using the wrong singular form, but Lady 4 Alligator still understood. 'My... name... is... *Ree-Ka*.'

It was like calling herself a tree or a squash, something which had no date of birth. Lady 4 Alligator waited politely. 'What is your name?' she asked again, still patient.

They discussed the question together again, and then the pale-haired one said, 'Eight Jaguar. I am Eight Jaguar.' She pointed to the other woman. 'She is Eleven Grass.'

Lady 4 Alligator smiled and wondered if they saw it in the flicker of the torchlight. 'Do you know why you are here?'

8 Jaguar began to cry again and the older 11 Grass said, 'Yes. Please release us.'

Lady 4 Alligator felt faintly shocked. 'Do you not know what sacrifice is?' There were those peoples who did not make such offerings, and they always had the hardest time accepting their role. Some of them never accepted it, and they screamed the whole time. 'Do your people not sacrifice?'

'Yes,' 11 Grass said haltingly, 'yes, our people do sacrifice. Our people –' she said a word that sounded like *vikingr* '– are much like your own. You call yourselves 'People of the Rain'; we sometimes call ourselves simply 'The People'. We also value bravery, and courage and war, and respect our gods with sacrifice, and are famous for our intricate metalwork, as are your folk. Yes, we sacrifice men. There are even those amongst us who sacrifice to a new god, and eat his flesh at every ceremony.' Lady 4 Alligator tried hard not to shudder with repulsion. 'But there are also those amongst us who do not believe in divine offerings, nor in human offerings, either.' And although her accent was strong, she used the Nasabi grammar fluently enough, and Lady 4 Alligator saw a seriousness in her strange eyes. Her jaw was set, and she did not tremble.

This is a warrior, Lady 4 Alligator realised, this is someone who does not quake for too long, even before death. And here I am, shivering just because I am afraid of appearing inexperienced for a ceremony.

'Have you fought in war?' she asked bluntly.

'We have,' said 11 Grass. But 8 Jaguar just stared grimly at Lady 4 Alligator.

11 Grass seemed resigned, and her speech came more quickly, as if nothing mattered now. 'You asked, so I will tell you that we are from a land so far away it is like it is in the sky itself. We travelled

Serpents, Corn and Honey

over water for months, and then we landed before winter in a new land. Over the next two years, we sailed along down the same coast with our crew. The weather grew hotter and more humid; occasionally we landed for food and camped. Then, nearly a year ago, we wrecked our vessel and some of us made it to land, and there was a great misunderstanding. Most of our surviving party were killed, including my sister.' 11 Grass's jaw shook, just for a moment. 'Myself and Ree... myself and Eight Jaguar were captured, and as the two survivors we were transported here to the stone mountains for this especial occasion, along with other captives from other regions of this land. We have learned your tongue during the last year. Yes, our people also burn and disembowel. We know why we are here. We have no illusions. Do not fool us with your interest and fake kindnesses, your smiles.'

Lady 4 Alligator was struck, violently, with sorrow. 'No,' she tried to explain, stepping closer, 'you will be honoured, like the boy of the broken flutes, with his beautiful maidens.' She reached out and put a hand softly on 11 Grass's shoulder.

'*Ree-ka*!' 11 Grass shouted out, and then Lady 4 Alligator was struggling; there was an arm round her neck, choking her, and a hand at her waist, removing her knife, and she was thrown back against the cold stone slab of the wall. She looked up at the two weird-eyed women, panting. They were already slicing through their bonds. She had been foolish to comfort them. She now realised that they must have had their hands free the entire time, and had lured her in here with their cries. She thought that they must have been waiting for just this opportunity. Yes, they would need knives, to fight their way out; they needed information as to which exits would be the safest. Then she thought of the shame 13 Vulture and her other brothers would feel, when she didn't show up for the banquet sacrifice, and the tears her mother would jet out, when her body was found inside the sacrifice corridor. What would people conjecture, as to how she got here? Well, it couldn't matter now.

She waited for a cut throat or death-blow similar to ones she'd delivered herself, and made her whole self into a gift for Qhuiyo, the goddess Lady 9 Reed. When it didn't come, she opened her eyes. They were looking at her and were arguing in low voices, in their prickly tongue.

11 Grass stepped forward. Her hair was not as dark, nor as shiny, as Lady 4 Alligator's own, not even in the torchlight. 'Eight Jaguar thinks you should be spared,' she said, her teeth glittering as white as the other woman's hair, 'she thinks you only tried to be kind to us. I am not as tender-hearted as she. I understand more of your thoughts. I think you are like all priests. You only think of duty, duty, duty. And rules, rules, rules.'

'That is not true,' Lady 4 Alligator was profoundly upset, 'I think well of the sacrifices. You are well fed and clothed. You are not something to be despised, like dirt or shit, but something to be honoured.'

She was starting to cry now too, she couldn't help it; cry like 8 Jaguar had before her. She had never felt so misunderstood, not even when she had told 13 Vulture that she wasn't sure she was up to the banquet sacrifice. And now she would die, and she would die misunderstood as well.

She sobbed, tears running down her neck, hot, reaching the collar of her tunic. She rose shakily to her feet.

'Stay where you are,' warned 11 Grass.

But Lady 4 Alligator didn't care if she were killed now; she stepped towards 11 Grass and 8 Jaguar. They did not lunge at her but shuddered away, and she tried to stretch out her arms; tried to hold them both in a great embrace where everything in the world was understood, where kind flesh spoke more clearly than the misunderstood complexities of language.

The older one grabbed Lady 4 Alligator's wrist as she tried to do this, though, and held it aloft and impotent in the air. 8 Jaguar made a sound that sounded like a reproach: *'Pee-ya!'* But yes, once again Lady 4 Alligator had failed to get her intentions across and it was probably the last time she would fail to do so, and she felt her heart being torn from her chest, that's what this pain felt like, such sorrow, and she fell on 11 Grass, with little warning, and she clasped the strange-eyed woman closer to her in desperation: human contact, the understanding she craved, the tenderness she had been hoping to show them in the first place, and she hugged 11 Grass to her, and she kissed her.

11 Grass pushed her off her immediately, a sharp shove, and Lady 4 Alligator stumbled backwards. The younger white-haired one was looking nearly as shocked as 11 Grass, at what Lady 4 Alligator had done.

Then the younger one said something in a harsh tone to 11 Grass, and moved forward to Lady 4 Alligator, supporting the priest in her arms. Lady 4 Alligator felt her fingers lightly on her tunic. She was comforting Lady 4 Alligator, patting her cheek, whispering unfamiliar words in her ear, putting her lips to her cheek, all in an effort to make her stop sobbing. Their faces were so close that they could feel the other's breath, and they were both kneeling, and both crying, and both had their hands cupped round the other's face. Lady 4 Alligator did not know when this intimacy changed to a kiss, but she did know that when it changed, like a grub to a butterfly, she felt like she were throwing off an encasement, sheer as a cocoon but as solid as stone. They were both still weeping. The stone-heavy weight broke off like an egg and 11 Jaguar and Lady 4 Alligator kissed and the Lady was free of her fear, free, free, free.

Like the spring ceremony for Xipe Tótec, Our Lord the Flayed One, free of his skin. Lady 4 Alligator shed her own, as a serpent does.

The white-haired woman's mouth was hot in the cool dampness of the sacrifice corridor. Her hands were fast on Lady 4

Alligator, beneath her tunic, as she rubbed them inside the priest, outside the priest, unsophisticated because she seemed so needy, and all the while 11 Grass watched them, and watched, and watched. Lady 4 Alligator mimicked 8 Jaguar, though she had no previous experience with women, for although the other woman's skin was strange it was still soft, and there was an odd beauty to her, Lady 4 Alligator had to admit it, with her old woman's hair and young woman's face, and her eyes which should be cataract-blind, by any logic, which saw the priest quite clearly enough. For 11 Jaguar sighed with delight when she touched Lady 4 Alligator's golden ear hangings with the little bells that jingled quietly, but did not attempt to steal them, and when the priest fondled her as she did the priest, she sighed again, and lifted up the tunic, so she could see better see the other woman's breasts.

Then, it all stopped. 8 Jaguar drew back. She was trying to say something to Lady 4 Alligator, but her words remained a mystery. That was when 8 Jaguar called 11 Grass over, and 11 Grass stood stiffly, with a grimace on her proud face, and 8 Jaguar took one of the older woman's hands and placed it over the priest's bare chest, just over her untorn heart, which still beat and beat. And then something seemed to melt 11 Grass's hardness at last, for Lady 4 Alligator understood, as she had from the beginning, that 11 Grass was a warrior in a way that the other one was not, that she had lived long enough – forty summers, by Lady 4 Alligator's estimate – to regret violence and still be toughened by it, a shell not unlike Lady 4 Alligator's own.

So when 11 Grass's composure cracked, Lady 4 Alligator was there already, and she let the other woman stroke her, and she stroked her in turn on her moon-pale skin, and she rubbed her fingers back and forth between her legs, over the little nub there. Then she put her fingers where the older woman was smoothest and moistest, far up inside her, to the same rhythm, while 11 Grass rubbed herself, and all the while the white-haired one was

Serpents, Corn and Honey

caressing the priest's rear – softly, like an eyelash, a butterfly – and flicking her tongue in between the priest's cheeks, just as lightly, so that Lady 4 Alligator credited 8 Jaguar with sophistication at last, and she could feel wetness running down her thighs, so wet was she.

And Lady 4 Alligator looked up on the carved walls – for it was not a prison, after all, but a place of tribute and honour, and she could see three carvings that stood out from amongst the mosaics and painted numbers and pearls as large as pigeon eggs, from amongst all the variety of beasts and vegetables and humans and nature. To her left, a pair of turquoise-eyed serpents; to the centre straight ahead an ear of maize, the kernels painted gold, blue, red and green; to her right, a bee, its abdomen dripping sensually – with honey. She shut her eyes and let them carry on.

For 11 Grass was groaning and thrusting herself towards the priest, her own hand strong on herself, and Lady 4 Alligator felt a pulsing deep within the other woman, on her wet fingers so tightly encased, and 8 Jaguar's flick-flick-flickering between the Lady's rear cheeks made her burn with pleasure, made her earrings jingle, and 11 Grass roared, and soon after so did 8 Jaguar, for it was then evident that the younger woman had been working on herself the whole time, and then the older woman called 11 Grass got down on her knees and licked between the priest's legs, fat big licks, over and over again until that sensation, combined with the flicker over Lady 4 Alligator's back-hole, snapped together into pleasure, and liquid ran down the priest's legs, and it was drunk up, and she groaned and grunted with the feeling.

It was fast, yes. Lady 4 Alligator looked around the alcove again, and saw the serpents, corn and honey. She wanted to discuss this with them, but they were panicking – even she, who spoke none of the language they squeaked out at each other, even she could hear this. So she did not tell them of the corn and honey and snakes; she did not tell them of the friezes and how danger, nourishment and sweetness added up to such pleasure. She told them, instead, of an unguarded exit, and the three of them embraced once, and then the other two were off.

As for herself, she ran past the further sacrifices, those who seemed content enough with their holy lot despite their feeble moans, and was out of the corridor and blinking in the light, running up the final step just as several guards, their pockets stuffed full of small flags, came down to collect the two sacrifices – the 'special' ones, meant for the ceremony.

She made it into the central area, moving rapidly past the common people and pushing her way through to where the dignitaries were, slipping herself down next to her younger brother on a woven mat just as the last minor prince with the royal plug bored through his nose declaimed his scripted piece, carefully following the vertical red guidelines that pointed out the story on the deerskin codex books.

'You fool, you could have made it very bad for yourself if you had not turned up,' 13 Vulture hissed at her, 'they have a pair of ghost-women to be split today, and all for you.' He looked at her closely. 'You don't seem nervous.'

'Why should I be?' Lady 4 Alligator picked up a small piece of avocado and put it in her mouth. It was creamy and delicious. She took a sip of cocoa, glanced around at the turquoise mosaics on the pillars and at those participants who wore masks of beaten gold, and let herself relax into the glamour and the ritual. For an instant, she felt an arm round her throat, someone lapping at her thighs, the faint echo of pleasure. She wasn't as late as she had feared. She hadn't even missed the meal.

There would be a problem when they couldn't find the ghost women. The guards would return from the corridor without the captives, captives who normally would be carrying the traditional small flag in each hand. The disappearance would be announced. And then she, Lady 4 Alligator, as if according to script, would rise to her feet and say that she had another tribute in mind for the altar. A burnt one. Of serpents, corn and honey. It was not unheard of, but there had to be some meaning attached to it, something that would give the substitution the weight of precious humanity, something worthy of a deity. The serpents are for danger, she would say, the corn is for nourishment and the honey is for sweetness. Now, what else does that remind you of?

And then they would consider this, priests, royals and crowd alike and, when they realised, Lady 4 Alligator would be hailed as a wise priest, and a natural, and her banquet sacrifice written down in every codex as the greatest of debuts.

The Case of the Cameo Rabbit

The Case of the Cameo Rabbit
Or, One Thick Dick

by Astrid Fox & Dr Stùpido

My name is Malloy. Rose Malloy. But all my friends call me Shifty. I used to have a career in law enforcement, but that damn doughnut allergy put a stop to that. All I have left now of those days are the memories of my pals in the force, some useful contacts, my little black notebook and a pair of standard issue handcuffs. I am a Dick now, earning my keep by pulling fast deals and even faster dames.

I'm going tell you a story, a tale of greed and corruption so sleazy it'll make your ears burn with scandal, your eyes pop out on stalks with disbelief, your tongue hang out your mouth from astonishment and your clit pulse with the hot, insistent throb of carnal jealousy. Because I hardly need to point out that not only do I usually get my man (not unlike the mounties), I get the women, too. So stop now if you can't bear to hear one dykely stud anecdote after another. Stop now if you're going to be so overcome with jealousy that you're going to start scanning the back-page ads of your old sex mags for clues and hints as to how you can reach the pinnacle of butch babehood that resonates from *moi*. Stop now, because let's face it: some of us have it, and some of us don't.

Better yet, read on and you might learn something...

It all began a week to the day before I got together with Catwoman. But first a bit about her.

Catwoman was definitely not my usual type, as her eyes were too close together. Still, there was something... provocative... in her stance and expression that fateful night, and I suddenly started to feel better about pulling dungeon duty at my local for the third evening running. (We have a backroom, sure, but it's a classy joint.)

That wasn't the only thing I hoped to be pulling that night.

She was standing close, close enough for me to notice the slightly uneven shave job, but far enough away to fake some composure if it turned out I needed it.

And if I were lucky it wouldn't be the only thing I was faking that night.

It soon became evident that I was going to need composure, artificial or nay. She turned around and those piercing brown eyes – which only moments ago had looked so close together – were looking straight at me, *perfectly spaced*. Why be so picky at closing time anyway? I ran my hand through my own dapper hair style – short top and sides, long in back, the mullet that all the girls go for.

Some murmured words, some implicit understanding that it wasn't the mild stuff I was digging tonight. A hand on her neck, a tongue at her ear, and we were together in the taxi. Wow. I'd done it. Again.

Kissing. Closely. I smelled her armpit, a musty mixture between cK One and sweat. Tugging my hair slightly with her teeth, she indicated her willingness for more. Wanting it. Desperate. I glanced at the cab driver, who was studiously ignoring the two of us, and thought better of it.

'Later, bitch,' I growled. My hand tightened on the worn crotch of my Levi 501s and I patted it appreciatively. She was dying to

The Case of the Cameo Rabbit

know if I was packing tonight, but I wasn't letting on.

The cab screeched to a stop outside my house. She offered to pay, and I let her. Then I unlocked my door and motioned Catwoman in. I let her walk up first (here's a tip for all you readers scanning my account for technique revelations: that way you get to check the babe out, and you also get to watch a new woman's reaction to your pad and your get-ups).

As I ascended, though, I inwardly cursed my lack of foresight in leaving those extra back copies of *Cosmo* lying around. My eyes lingered on the sway of her hips as she walked up to the second level. I idly wondered what sort of piercings she'd be hiding under that diamanté catsuit she was wearing.

We entered to the familiar smell of Fahrenheit For Men and pussy.

'Hey, you don't mind if I feed my pet first?' I mumbled. I retreated with a dish into the kitchen, fervently hoping the naff endearments necessary to pacify the hungry Tiffany wouldn't be overheard by the even more delectable dish waiting in the front room. While pouring out milk with my right hand, I poured out two stiff brandies with my left hand (talented, yes, I know – that's what all the girls say). I stifled an impulse to call out and ask her alcoholic preference.

Dames don't like to be asked. They like to be told.

'I hate brandy.' She faced me with a steely look that would set some of my more stony friends to stripping off their boxer shorts and running for the lube. 'Get me a coffee. Black. No sugar.'

Women.

When I returned – surreptitiously stirring the Nescafé with my pinky – I saw she had taken the liberty of pulling down a fair amount of the magazines from the top of the curio cabinet and was now leafing through them on the sofa-bed. I moved in slowly. In control now, I set the coffee down on the bedside table and took the magazines away from her, as if from a child. 'I don't think you'll be needing these right now, will you,' I murmured, my teeth just inches away from her neck.

There was a pause.

'Is that so?' The phrase was hissed out between the pressure valves of her lips. 'We'll see about that.'

Knowing that this must be the signal that we'd both been waiting for, I stripped naked as fast as I could and flopped back down on the sheets of the bed. With admirable foresight, I grabbed a pillow and propped my head up, opening my legs as far apart as they would go. That would save her the trouble of having to reach for the pillow later and messing up her rhythm. I sighed happily in anticipation. Why did she have to wait so long? If she had dawdled much longer, I might actually have had to make the first move myself.

I opened one eye. Catwoman was staring at me, in what looked like shock. Then she shook her head – why? – swiftly pulled on a glove retrieved from the depths of her ladylike purse, doused it with lube (an economy-size bottle, also found in the purse) and started fucking me like there was no tomorrow.

Suddenly, my mind was inundated with images of waterfalls, the raging ocean, Anna Nicole Smith, and I was a wet tiger, a roaring wet tiger, fringed black leather jackets –

'I'm a tiger!' I screamed, 'I'm a tiger, aren't I? Call me a tiger!' – rockets soaring, limpid pools, Uma as Venus, Kylie's bum, Barbarella, Cleo Rocos, Ann Summer's Fall Collection and Oh! I Was One!

That night we were not divided.

I experienced things I had never experienced before, and I think she did, too, if her slight, ironic smirk was anything to judge by. Afterwards, Tiffany scratched outside and moonlight flickered in through the venetian blinds while Catwoman dozed...

Cigarette in my mouth, I again lay flat on my back, stared up at the ceiling and smoked.

The Case of the Cameo Rabbit

A moment passed. Then two. The dame was distracting, I'd give her that. But I had my own problems to sort through and not even that sparkle off her second molar could shine them away. Why was this always the case? I asked myself, looking down at her sumptuous body.

I knew the answer.

A bird could never supply me with the answers; she could only complicate them. From the Rimmel-lipped babes on the city's rough side to the slick city women in their rough cashmere sweaters, women existed to cause trouble.

Women's trouble.

And now I was in trouble, too. As I lay on the bed there with Catwoman, I mused back to the events of the week before, when a different smoky-eyed beauty had wobbled up to me in my local bar-cum-freelance office.

I took another drag off my cigarette. What had her name been, anyway? She certainly hadn't the obvious charms of the tart trixie in bed beside me now. Hers was a more subtle appeal and her appeal to me – 'Please help me...' – was subtle, too.

That's right, that's where it had all begun, six days previous at the Queen Anne's Index Finger.

I had been drinking heavily and the smoky-eyed girl – her name was Leila, she had said, now it was all coming back to me – had waltzed over to me in fringed red suede cowboy boots. But really tasteful ones, right? Right from the beginning, I thought it had to be a set-up. I could see a glowering mountain of a butch watching from a side table as Leila moved in closer, her breath as smoky as her eyes and cigarettes.

She smoked Super-Kings and so do I.

'Please help me,' she whispered. She moved still closer. 'My girlfriend...' A slight nod of her soft chin towards the dangerous and depressed-looking thug at the table. Now, I make it a point never to get involved in lovers' quarrels, but I do hate to see a damsel in distress. Even though distress was never a private thing in *this* bar. For example, from the corner a baby-dyke was weeping about her new cat's bleeding ears, if my own ears didn't deceive me. And in front of me, a woman at the pool table was screeching about an unfair shot and was brandishing a cue in an unfriendly manner. But soon all eyes in the room were focused in our direction; I could see the swing of many earrings, the shimmer of sequins, the dull glare of corduroy as bodies moved closer in an attempt to eavesdrop.

People had even stopped listening to an interesting-looking couple squabbling in the corner, a pair who wore matching silver shellsuits and Stetsons.

Yep, it had all been only six days ago and, in the aftermath of that conversation with Leila, I'd come up with *nada*.

The most action I'd had in a week now lay stretched out before me on the bed asleep, her lips faintly glistening, her bits strangely dry. Didn't she have a good time? Oh, well. I put it out of my mind. I took another drag. Yep, the girl next to me had tricks up her sleeve, all right. Made me think I should pick up a copy of the old Karma Chameleon Sutra. That removal-of-socks thing needed more looking into. She was so insistent. Matter of fact, now that I thought about it, she looked distinctly familiar. That little gold brooch on the sash of the diamanté catsuit, now strewn on the floor...

Ah yes – more than just strange coincidence. I had indeed seen that catsuit before, that same night last week at the bar with Leila... The babe on the bed had been there in the hub-bub of the masses. Now I clearly remembered the shimmer of her outfit from that listening crowd, the diamanté amongst the other punters' sequins, satin, ostrich feather hair-clips... Had she heard the

The Case of the Cameo Rabbit

conversation that followed?

I don't think so.

Tiffany continued to scratch outside, and Catwoman continued snoring, but I managed to ignore them both. I had bigger fish to fry, so I took another drag and tried to recall more details of that night.

Leila had whispered slowly, almost languorously in my ear, almost wetly. 'You see my girlfriend over there...'

I looked over and gave a masterful nod to the butch in the corner. She had a certain She-Hulkian charm, even I had to admit it.

'She's asked me to come talk to you... you see, she doesn't want to appear to be asking herself. She's shy that way.'

Well, I reassured Leila I wouldn't give the game away immediately and a half-hour or so later, when the focus was off me and on a switchblade fight by the A-Team pinball machine, I sauntered over to them, carrying a pint of Jägermeister for the girl and a parasoled raspberry Midori colada for the hulk. Threesome-o-rama, I thought. I had nothing against multiple fun, and obviously my name in the bar had become synonymous with 'good time'.

They both cooed grateful thank-yous and took their drinks, then sat embarrassed for several seconds until they broke the silence at the same time.

'You see, Charlene and I...' That was from Leila.

'Leila needs –' From Charlene. They both broke off, and looked at me helplessly.

'Well, spit it out, girls,' I said.

'Oh, damn it, Charlene, just let me do the talking,' said Leila. She looked at me. 'It's a trifle mortifying, but after I say it, I think we'll all feel better, won't we? You see, Charlene has this notion she can't be topped.'

'Topped?' I was puzzled.

'You know, flipped. Mastered in bed. By a femme.'

'But isn't that how it always... oh, never mind.' I took out my little black notebook and ruffled through the address section. 'I've got to tell the two of you, the pimping business is not for me. But if you hold on a second, I can provide you with a couple of numbers and recommendations.'

'No, no, no, you don't understand,' interrupted Leila. Charlene was nearly in tears. 'We can provide for ourselves, thank you very much. As a matter of fact, that's part of the problem. We ran a rather – dare I say it – *provocative* ad two weeks ago in the paper and we have just received oodles of scrumptious replies. The problem is that a *threat* ran in the paper the very next week, before we even had the chance to reply to *any* of them.' She handed over a pile of newspaper clippings, the first one of which read:

TWO RAMBUNCTIOUS BUNNIES, 1 'BLUE' AND 1 'PINK', SEEK
JESSICA-RABBIT TYPE TO DOMINATE, CONTROL AND
MISTRESS BUNNY BLUE. PHOTOS PLEASE.

The second clipping was more ominous.

BUNNIES. IF YOU GO THROUGH WITH YOUR
COUPLINGS OR TRIPLINGS, IT COULD MEAN STEW.
FATAL ATTRACTIONS CAN BE STICKY.

'Hmm,' I said. 'Did you get any photos sent with the first bunch?' As I rubbed my thighs together surreptitiously under the table, Leila handed over three photographs.

'Most of them didn't send photos, after all,' she admitted. 'But their *descriptions* were absolutely *delicious*.'

'Have the two of you, uh, followed through?' I queried. They shuffled their feet.

'No,' piped up Leila. 'Charlene's been too scared. You see, it

The Case of the Cameo Rabbit

takes an awful lot for Charlene to admit this need anyway, to be vulnerable in this way, and this just spooked us far too much. Didn't it, Cottontail?'

Charlene grimaced.

I looked at them both. Bunny Pink and Bunny Blue, sitting there together in perfect harmony. 'I charge,' I said, finally. 'There's always a price attached. And I need expenses.'

'Of *course* you do,' purred Leila. 'And we're willing to pay, aren't we, Char-Char?' Charlene grunted her assertion and handed over a wad of bills.

'And I'm going to need all the correspondence, I'm afraid, Leila.'

Leila grudgingly relinquished a knapsack crammed full of perfumed letters, which I received with damp, eager palms.

'I even received jewellery, anonymously,' giggled Leila, showing me a locket with an unusual cameo of a carved rabbit head. I admired it briefly, gathered up the bulk of things and told them I'd be in contact same time, same place next week.

Nope. I'd had absolutely no leads. None of the photos checked out – at least there were no girls that I knew and no girls that looked like they might fancy me – and even after a laborious handwriting sample analysis of the letters (there was a booth that did it for two quid at the Dalston Mall), it had all been a no-go. I had no idea what I was going to tell the two of them tomorrow.

Aw, but what did any of that have to do with the luscious vixen I now found stretched before me, spread-eagled – if only in sleep – on my bed.

On the floor, her brooch positively sparkled in the moonlight.

I bent closer.

I could just barely make out the glint of a perky cameo rabbit head. I shuddered. While I had been rattling on in an internal dialogue, the clues had been right before me. Things were getting hare-y, all right.

*

I must have dozed off again. Sunlight was pouring in through the windows like thick honey on waffles. Something was wrong; I felt it in my bones.

I looked around, trying to make sense of what it was that I couldn't put my finger on, when my glance fell on the alarm clock by my side.

Damn! I was late for my side-line job at the Cat Lovers' Institute! The babe had departed during the night. In my time as the Donna Juan of Hackney, I have learned that it is usually this way, and I have learned to accept it. I mused for a moment on what it would be like to actually have a woman still in bed with me when morning came, but I didn't have time for such philosophical ruminations, because I was quickly slipping into my denims and T-shirt, throwing some reduced-calorie Iams for Tiffany – who was nowhere to be seen – into her bowl and racing out the door.

Moira tapped her fingers on one of the cat baskets when I turned up nearly an hour late. 'What time you call this?' she croaked. 'You could have been caught in a bombing raid.'

As sweet as Moira was, she was also completely off her rocker. A while ago a bombing campaign against a famous vivisectionist went wrong, and since then she thinks she's back in 1943. But crazy or not, she could still remember all the names of the 267 cats that were in residence.

As penance, I went to work immediately cleaning the cat litter trays. After two hours' hard graft, Moira called me in to take a quick tea break. She insisted on dispensing a cup of tea and a slice of cake each time I was round – 'You never know, it might be your last one – a doodlebug could hit you any minute.'

She proffered me the dark brown liquid and a piece of Battenberg this time, which was a bit of a treat. Doughnuts had been a problem when I was in the force, but I had no allergy to this particular delicacy.

'I got a letter from Arthur from the front this morning,' she began.

Uh-oh. She was usually in a bad state when she talked of her long-dead husband.

'He says he's sure that he will be home by Christmas and not to worry. Food's all right, but he told me he won't eat rabbit no more unless it's got its head on. This bloke from his company made a rabbit stew, only it turned out to be cat. Apparently, you can't tell cat and rabbit apart unless by the tail and the head.' She went on like that for a while, talking about the stress of rationing and so forth, while I finished my tea.

'Well, Moira, duty calls.' I liked listening to her talk about the old days but I also had to earn some money. After all, Moira had insisted that I got paid per cleaned cat litter tray, and there were three cats per tray.

During lunchtime I decided that the brooch that Leila and Charlene had been sent via Royal Mail was the key to the whole matter, not the letters or the photographs, and that it needed some serious investigation. I checked all the antique shops in my little black book, describing the details over the phone. To no avail. My leads had dried up, it seemed.

Leila and Charlene's troubles were still playing on my mind when I took the bus back home in the early afternoon. Clocking a dame in the seat before me, I leaned closer to smell her perfume. Ah, nothing's quite like Charlie. Classy and absolutely my type. Not that I was that fussy anyway. I tried to see what her profile looked like and leaned out slightly to the side. Disappointed with studenty glasses, I sat back in my seat. I had nearly given up on my prey when I spotted the article she was reading:

Astrid Fox

CATS ARE THE TRUE CONQUERORS OF THE WORLD
BY PROF. LAGOMORT

After decade-long investigations into the habits and genetics of the common rabbit, it has now been conclusively shown that they are in fact only malformed cats. 'With the use of plastic surgery it is now possible to give back normal looks to these poor disadvantaged cats, which allows them to lead happy, useful lives. Furthermore, it will mean that they can finally be fully integrated into the cat family,' says a proud Professor Lagomort. This major scientific breakthrough is hotly tipped to receive the Nobel...

Unfortunately at that point the dame got up abruptly to leave the bus. Looking up – just to make doubly sure that she wasn't my type – my mouth fell open: it was the woman from last night! Rushing after her, I got off the bus only to see her walk into a building buzzing with people coming and going – the Institute for Biological Research. I raced through the door of this imposing, monolithic edifice.

But she was gone.

I turned around for some clue – any clue. Near the lifts, I found the office directory of the Institute. And Professor Lagomort's name was top of the list. Even above Professor Alice Aaronson's.

A zinger went off like an electric bomb in my head at this point. Catwoman – the Professor – the brooch – Leila's cameo locket...

Why hadn't I seen it before? It was so obvious!

It was Catwoman – or rather, Speccy – I needed to talk to. Maybe she could provide a link between the two cameo rabbit heads and thus give me a lead on this Fatal Attraction-esque case – you see, I found it strangely obsessive that someone would send a locket to a complete stranger and I suspected a foul connection. Even though I hadn't made the connection until now, the pieces

The Case of the Cameo Rabbit

to the puzzle had been there simmering in my head all the time, jumbled up like a mixed metaphor.

Meanwhile, I'd have to curb my distaste for eyeglasses and get back on Catwoman's good side, so to speak.

There she was, stepping into the lift! I briskly managed to squeeze in beside her, just as the door closed. We were the only two in the lift and her back was to me. I decided to use the full thrust of my charm. Breathing heavily – she was pretending, coyly, to ignore me – I approached from behind, as is my wont, and then ripped the glasses from her face in a single, fluid movement.

'Why, Miss Mystery,' I murmured, 'you're beautiful.'

And she was, damn it.

'You again.' It was a chilly statement; Miss Mystery Catwoman sounded curiously underwhelmed. I handed the specs back in the ensuing stony silence, as she seemed to expect that I would do so. She put them on immediately. 'How dare you?' she added, unkindly, 'I can't see a thing without these – even if there happened to be something worth seeing.' She sniffed and turned around again.

She dug me, all right. I could tell.

Also, I had made the clever observation while the glasses were still in my hand that they were, in a word, 'attitude glasses'. That is to say, they were non-prescription pure glass. Catwoman didn't need them at all. But why was she wearing them? And to what purpose?

As far as I'm concerned, Scary Spice alone can wear specs and wear them well. Anastacia comes a poor second. And as for all the others who make their attempts, I'm afraid that Dorothy Parker put it best: Shifty Malloy don't make passes at dames who wear glasses. I find spectacles execrable. A Fashion Crime. A Real Turn-Off. And now, they were adding up to a puzzle for which I didn't have the piece, simmering in my synapses or not. See previous simile, readers, if you're confused.

Fortunately, I remembered my original mission. 'Look, honey,

I'm sorry I grabbed your glasses.' I laid on the charm real thick. 'It's just hard sometimes trying to get the attention of a pretty lady like yourself. And I wanted to ask you a couple questions –'

She interrupted with a stiff smile. 'I think it's best, don't you, that we just draw a long dark shroud over the whole episode that was last night and never speak of it again. That would save us both, particularly me, a great deal of embarrassment. And now, if you'll excuse me, this is my floor.'

The lift had stopped on the thirteenth floor and, as the light with the number 13 on it glowed weakly in a dull, fluorescent, yet still indicatory manner, I stepped forward and momentarily stopped the doors from fully opening and Mystery Kitty from exiting.

'Perhaps,' I said smoothly, 'you will be interested in this little trinket.' I drew from my pocket the small locket that Leila had given me, its exquisitely carven rabbit's head winking in the track lighting of the lift.

Catwoman, en route to brush past me, paused and drew in a breath as her pupils grew dilated, filling up most of her masked, albeit lovely, irises. Suddenly she removed her left hand from the pocket of her slacks, where it had been up to this point, raised it quickly and, with talon-like precision, her fingernails administered three long parallel scratches on my cheek. She exited whilst I still stood paralysed in shock. The door of the lift shut and I found myself again on the ground floor. I stepped out into the lobby again, nursing my wounds. Funny how I hadn't noticed those nails the night before.

She must have been right-handed.

'So I'm sorry,' I concluded to Leila and Charlene after they had bought me a Pink Lady with Blue Curacao ice cubes, 'but it's going to take me a bit longer than expected. This is a complicated case. A real complicated case. A real complicated, *expensive* case.'

Charlene sighed and handed over another wad of bills,

The Case of the Cameo Rabbit

which I swiftly pocketed. 'Do what you have to do,' she said, 'the situation can only improve.'

'You mean –'

'Things have become much worse,' squealed Leila, 'another warning appeared in the paper today. Here...'

I quickly grabbed the newspaper and scanned the Personals. I used to do this regularly, and even got a few dates out of the whole thing but, after four or five complaints from my blind dates, the Personals Editor refused to allow me to advertise or respond any more. Since this happened, I've always had a bit of a grudge against the paper. So I don't keep up with it like I used to: nevertheless, this development gave me a chance to quickly peruse the talent I'd been missing during my hiatus.

'Feline owner seeks free advice regarding new kitten's skull disease... Cool blonde femme seeks hirsute Britney Spears lookalike for punishment beatings... Dapper fop seeks similar for peacocking about... hmm, that's not so bad – I might have to give that butch/butch stuff a whirl one of these days... Gorgeous black sex-kitten longs for foamy, long baths and one naughty girl to share them with... HEL-lo! That's a good one, isn't it?' I noticed that both Charlene and Leila were staring at me glumly and I hurriedly scanned down the rest of the page. 'Ah yes, here we are: BAD BUNNIES. THE WALLS HAVE EARS (THOUGH THE TWO OF YOU WON'T, IF YOU KEEP IT UP). DO YOURSELVES A FAVOUR AND DROP THE DICK.' I cleared my throat. 'I take it that means me.'

At this point I had to take matters into my own hands. I took as my motto one of the ramblings Moira was always muttering under her breath whenever she was having a funny turn: 'Attack on two fronts'. So I did exactly that. I placed an ad in the Personals myself due to run the next day in the *Hackney Mumble*. This is how it read:

BIG BAD BUNNY WITH DARING DAY-JOB
AS DASHING DETECTIVE BEGS BUSTY BELLIGERENT BABE
TO TREAT ME REAL REAL BAD
BOX # 1234

It wasn't the first time I had begged, but it was the first time I'd done it publicly. Okay, fifth time. Still, it wasn't like any of my pals would recognise me and, as far as bait went, I figured it would do the trick.

My next plan of attack was more difficult to fix and it took a few hours to sort out. First I made a phone call to Swizzlestick Temp Agency, where a pal of mine worked.

'Harry! How are ya?'

'Not so bad, Shifty, not so bad... How's tricks?'

Harry held a grudge from the days back in the force when the ladies in the line-up always fell for me and not for him. I told him at the time, that's the way the cookie crumbles. He might have a green streak but he was sound.

'I need a job, Harry.'

He relished the moment. 'I wondered when you'd get your sorry ass out of that pub and off the dole.'

'No, I need a *specific* job, Harry. Namely at the Institute for Biological Research.'

'It'll cost ya.'

'Never thought it wouldn't, Harry.'

The photocopier machine operator at the Institute for Biological Research – now languishing at St Mary's General Hospital – never felt a thing. As for me, I showed up promptly at 8.57am on the thirteenth floor of the Institute in my American Tan stockings, side-split skirt and freshly cropped mullet. It had taken a lot of pancake to cover up the scratches on my face, but even so the male receptionist winked at me when I walked in. When you got it, you got it.

The Case of the Cameo Rabbit

I was soon handed a foot-high stack of papers by a man whose cravat screamed Middle Management. 'We don't fuss with those new-fangled staple-openers at the Institute,' he told me. 'We're traditional here. Take the staples out first,' he informed me very patiently and extremely slowly, 'you do this by first opening each end of the metal staple – which is folded – with your fingernails. Then, slowly pull the staple through the holes that run through the sheets and by then you'll have removed it successfully. Then you can throw that staple away – don't worry about refolding the metal ends again – and start on the next stapled stack. Do you understand?'

It was a puzzler, but eventually I got the hang of it, and knew that it wasn't going to be too long before they gave me an opportunity to use the actual photocopier – maybe even before the end of the day, if my learning curve kept on soaring to such stratospheric heights.

As I settled into to a bend-pull-pluck routine, I let my eyes wander around the open-plan office, wondering where I could possibly start to look for clues. I held a hand up to my cheek, where the scratches still stung, then lowered it to finger the turquoise-green polyester collar of my outfit. I felt peculiar in a blouse and skirt, but drag was drag and work was work. The tights were damn itchy, though, and I found myself reaching up with one hand to adjust the gusset whilst simultaneously removing the staples from the sheaf of documents all stamped CONFIDENTIAL. It was at this moment I met the eye of a woman I recognised from the framed photo-directory at Reception – the Vice-President of the Institute, a stunning blonde corporate lady who appeared to be watching me with a look of fascination and horror. Then her eyes narrowed, and she smoothed the lapel of her Marks & Spencer suit and moved towards me. Then she was near breathing down my neck. I swear it.

'First day?' she murmured. She reached her hands around either side of my beskirted elastic waistband. 'Here, let me show you an easier way.'

I knew her type, right off. She was the kind of corporate ballbreaker who likes to take advantage of naïve young work replacement girls just new to big business.

'See, just bend the flaps aside, gently, and then push your finger against it, with a regular pressure. There, that's it.'

I found myself breathing in time to her, as I followed her instructions.

'You're so pretty,' she whispered in my ear, before biting the lobe with a quick sharp nip.

'Ow!'

'You're so pretty and feminine,' she continued, seducing me with her fine low voice and her scent of Wella Balsam Hair Conditioner, 'I do so like a girl who looks like a girl. None of those tomboys with their dungarees and cropped hairstyles.' She made a staple pop off in a millisecond with a flick of her long varnished fingernail. I watched its trajectory; it landed on the grey carpet, where it sparkled underneath the fluorescent track lighting.

'Never mind about that,' she murmured, massaging my breasts, which trembled under my frilly blouse, 'such a lovely big girl's blouse this is. Just lovely. So womanly. And your hair – well, it's *half*-long, I guess anyway. Have you ever considered curling tongs?'

'Yes,' I admitted, wanting at the same time to defend my butch ego but Silly Putty in her hands; her hands which tweaked at my nipples all the same, 'curling tongs, crimpers, Barbie Doll Brand eyeshadow, you name it,' I babbled, traitor to my tomboy sistas but loving it, loving her corporate slut hands, yes, yes, yes, yes.

She stopped fondling me suddenly and I gasped with disappointment.

'Follow me,' she said, taking me by the hand and leading me towards the photocopier.

'But I'm not ready for that yet,' I murmured feebly but still grabbing my stapling assignment with my free hand and letting myself be led by her strong businesswoman's grip towards the photocopying alcove, 'they said maybe by late afternoon, if I worked hard at my de-stapling...' My voice trailed off as she directed me to the Xerox machine and I sighed a deep throaty moan of desire. She opened up the lid of the photocopier, and set it on manual. I groaned again.

'Do it, darling,' she whispered, 'do it for me.'

I dropped my stapling assignment with CONFIDENTIAL in big bold letters written at the top of every page and gave in then, gave in to the sensation of her fingers round my waist as she pushed and heaved me up, up, up. I shut my eyes. I felt the cold glass on the bottom of my thighs.

Carefully, reverently, she then began to unroll my American Tan tights.

'You, you... slut!' She stopped for a moment, seemingly shocked by the fact that I was wearing no underwear. I moaned even louder then to remind her of the task at hand, and it was then that I felt the whole machine vibrate, as she pushed the green START button and I felt the whir underneath me, and the electric flash of lights beneath my thighs as she photocopied my butt.

'Oh yes,' I sighed, as she set the machine for 10 copies, then a big A3 size, 'oh yes, yes.' In my ecstasy I was barely aware of my corporate goddess frotting herself up against the photocopier as it emitted a steady vibrato under my own straining weight. I felt the delicate sensibility that comes from pure exhibitionism, from erotic titillation as opposed to quick-and-dirty wham-bam. It occurred to me that I was finally getting in touch with my feminine side. I opened my eyes with the realisation – the suited woman still rubbing herself energetically against the machine now spewing out copy after copy of my butt, reduced 10%, enlarged 35%, photo-mode, fax-mode, 120 copies a minute – and I met the eye of Catwoman herself across the alcove, also dressed in a corporate suit, and staring at my naked-butted self sitting moaning with pleasure, being pawed by the Vice-President of the Institute, and brushing my floppy mullet off my sweaty neck as well as the foundation that was dripping down my face, staring at me in my extreme femme drag. Once again, she looked a little shocked.

I could just barely make out the words her lips were mouthing: 'You! Again!'

I winked at her, but it was difficult to project my customary suavité in my position and, besides, the Vice-President was winding up. In the interim, Catwoman and I stared each other out in a game of 'who'll blink first'. Then I realised Catwoman wasn't actually staring at me – she was staring at the pile of unstapled papers I'd dropped, now spread all over the floor, each with a CONFIDENTIAL or PRIVATE or SECRET stamped on front. The penny dropped. I slid off the machine. The moment seemed frozen. At last, the Vice-president vibrated herself to a final 'Oh!' on the sort-tray and a curious silence came over the alcove as the whir of the photocopier at last drew to a close as well.

The Vice-President seemed suddenly to come to her senses. She hastily smoothed down her skirt. She didn't even look me in the eye as she snapped, 'Clean this mess up!' and stalked out of the enclosure.

For a few clean seconds, the frozen moment continued, and Catwoman and I stared at each other for real this time. I was aware of a tic in my left eye, but I didn't let it throw me. Tic, tic. Time passed. Tick, tick. Tic, tick. Tick, tic.

The moment passed. We both made a dive for the stapling assignment at the same time. I suddenly saw the words RESEARCHED BY PROF. LAGOMORT on every single spilled sheet and cursed myself for not having noticed that before during my three hours of manual staple removal.

I was closer, and rose up from the struggle flourishing the documents.

The Case of the Cameo Rabbit

'Give me those!' Catwoman tried to make a grab for the papers, and succeeded.

But I was valiant, and grabbed them straight back. 'Hands off, lady!' I kept my distance as we circled, though, remembering the talons of her left hand and the scratches I still wore. She made a final desperate swoop, but I dodged her, and there was a clatter as her specs fell to the ground.

'They didn't do you any favours anyway, sweetie,' I hissed at her, clutching the stapling assignment to my chest.

'Nor does the get-up you're in now,' she spat out in an equally low voice.

'Okay, lady, I know the glasses aren't real. Now why don't you fess up and tell me why you're so interested in Professor Lagomort's research?'

'Why don't you tell ME why you're so interested?' she returned. 'You don't even work here. That's the crummiest disguise I've ever seen.'

'Sister, you don't work here either,' I pointed out, and it was here that I put my observation skills on full dazzling display: 'You don't have the right colour of plastic sheath for your company name-tag.'

Catwoman glanced down at her left breast, and I indulged myself in a good long look as well. She seemed to swallow back some words, then whispered, 'Okay, you got me.' She was still looking longingly at my stapling assignment and I edged away a bit. 'Where can we go to talk in private? I think we need to blow this pop-stand.'

'I think you need to blow something else,' I joked, but she didn't seem to understand. 'I'll meet you at the Queen Anne's Index Finger in fifteen minutes,' I said, 'but you leave first, so no one gets suspicious.'

I made my own way out quite casually, stapling assignment

shoved deep into my handbag, with a bright 'toodle-loo!' and a wave to the appreciative young man on reception. He must have been choking on his low-fat Boots-own-brand cheese & onion crisps, because I could have sworn it sounded like he was snickering. Or maybe he was just shy – people get that way around me, guys and gals alike.

'I'm going to level with you,' said Catwoman, 'my name is Regina, and I'm actually a private investigator for the Lowbush Moose Agricultural Club of Chelmsford. I took on a case to puzzle out why the meadow populations of certain animals such as field mice and rabbits have fallen to such lows this year in Hackney Marshes. It's got me really worried, and so when I saw a significant advertisement in the *Hackney Mumble* about bunnies, I placed another one to warn the couple, just in case they too were targeted by this mad field-mouse and rabbit fiend. I thought I might find out more information at the Institute for Biological Research, since I'd just read an article that they have a world-famous animal expert working there – Professor Lagomort.'

'Ah, that explains the second ad.' I bobbed my head up and down in a sage manner, and quickly talked Regina through my own role, as well as informing her about the third decoy ad I'd placed. Regina just nodded throughout, and seemed strangely dismissive of the night we had spent together, almost as if she were politely trying to change the subject.

'Well, we've got at least two good potential leads.' She smiled a patient smile and withdrew the day's copy of the *Hackney Mumble* out of her own handbag at the same time as I brought forth the stapling assignment. We both scanned our respective papers quickly, and both cried 'Eureka!' at the same time.

'Look, here! A haiku!' She briskly pointed out a new Personals ad, which read: 'I LIKE BAD BUNNIES/ BUT ARE THEY CLEVER ENOUGH/ TO KNOW MY OWN PLAN.'

The Case of the Cameo Rabbit

'No, read this –!' I quoted: '"Biography, Professor Lagomort: not only an esteemed scientist, but a great lover of Japanese traditional poetry, which the Professor likes to compose at home, on 1234 Mulberry Street!"'

We looked at each other. 'Eureka!' we both cried together, in chorus this time. I tried to put my arm around Regina in the impassioned fellow feeling of the moment, but she wouldn't let me.

Mulberry Street was quiet as we walked along the houses, making our way towards 1234. It didn't help matters that we started out at No. 1. All the time I was heavily aware of Regina's strong gait, the beautiful curve of her hips and all the words her name could rhyme with. Haikus are fine, but I prefer a standard A/B/C/B pattern.

When we got there, we could see a stooped-over figure bumbling around inside. The Professor. No doubt drawing inspiration for the next poem, or plotting evil deaths for poor field mice. There was a strong, familiar scent as we walked up the pathway to the door, but I couldn't quite place it.

As Regina leant in to push the doorbell, my feelings were near uncontrollable. 'Hands off,' she muttered through gritted teeth, as the door slowly, slowly began to open.

It was Moira, from the Cat Lovers' Institute!

For once, Shifty Malloy was caught off-guard. 'But... but I don't understand!'

Moira began to cackle evilly, in her own peculiar mad way. 'Well, are you coming in or not?' she snapped.

Regina was just gaping. I decided to take charge of matters: 'Where is Professor Lagomort?'

'I *am* Professor Lagomort!' Moira screeched. Not Moira the doodlebug lady! I was genuinely shocked. We pushed past Moira into the darkened house, and in the dismal light thrown by one study lamp we saw dozens of pathetic creatures hopping around, all with very short ears.

'Oh no!' Regina was tearful, and fell straight to her knees, trying to hug as many of the furry creatures to her beautiful bosom as she could.

'That's right,' Moira was muttering in her lovably nutty way, 'as I told Arthur last night, you've got to keep up appearances. I saw *two* messages in code this week alone in the *Hackney Mumble*, and this reminded me that if we don't persevere with the good fight, the War will be all but lost...'

'What?' I was staring first at Moira, then at the sobbing Regina. 'What's going on?'

'Don't you get it, you fool?' (There was no call for Regina to be nasty, in my opinion.) 'She wants to cut the ears off ALL the rabbits! She uses plastic surgery! She even fed the field mice to the horrible felines! She uses the dyke community's well-known love of cats as a cover!'

'Moira? Is this true?'

But Moira was whispering to herself again, a subdued raspy monologue about stew and Arthur and cats and rabbits.

Regina, still teary-eyed, rose to her feet with a great sigh. 'She doesn't understand, Shifty. She's a brilliant yet nefarious professor, but the brilliance comes and goes, and so does the wickedness – when she's at the Cat Lovers' Institute, she's just a kind kooky old woman whose love of cats goes a little too far. When she's Professor Lagomort, bad things happen and gentle innocent creatures get hurt. She thought those personal ads from your clients were a throwback to the war days – and in code – and it just triggered something in her. The best thing we can do is force her hand at an early retirement, and then keep a close eye on her at the Cat Lovers' Institute to ensure that she does not commit further evil on poor innocent bunnies.'

'But how do you know all this?

The Case of the Cameo Rabbit

Regina rose to her full height, which admittedly was a good half-foot on me. 'I couldn't tell you this before, Shifty, but I am a member of a counter-intelligence movement. As I told you before, I placed the second ad. That's true. But I also sent the rabbit-head cameo to Leila and Charlene as a protective amulet, a warning against vigilantes from the Institute for Biological Research, for even *they* don't want to mess with my... organisation. Which must remain unnamed. I went deep under cover, Shifty – too deep. Our night together was pure business. I can't stress that enough. I like my girls a bit more polished, no offense. What's more, I hate cats – I can't stand the creatures, and particularly not your ugly smelly Tiffany, by the way. I'm really a rabbit lover. I have raised the gentle beasts since I was a girl of ten. I infiltrated the lesbian-cat-plastic-surgery community, spearheaded by Professor Moira Lagomort. And you know what? It's all been worth it. I feel pleased now. If one more rabbit gets to keep its ears and avoids looking like a malformed cat, I will sleep easy at night.'

I let her bluster on for a while and then it hit me that the Case of the Cameo Rabbit was, for all practical purposes, sorted. Thinking of the big bonus I'd be getting from Leila and Charlene, I swaggered a little closer to Regina. Her lovely, pointy bosoms were mouth-level. I felt my throat go dry. I stroked the rabbit-foot I always kept in my pocket for luck, and I leaned in close to Regina, knowing full well that she was savouring the moment as much as I was.

'I'm ready when you are,' I whispered in her ear. I was breathing huskily and it was turning me on, as well as her.

Regina flinched and drew away from me, staring at me with that look of horror I'd come to realise was her 'coy' look. 'I rather think not, Shifty. I rather think not.' She gathered as many rabbits into her arms as she could and made her way out the door, leaving me on my ownsome and Moira gibbering in a corner.

I thought hard for about two seconds, and then I made my

Astrid Fox

way back towards the Queen Anne's Index Finger. I squared my shoulders before I exited, though, and winked at Moira in a friendly, spirit-of-the-Blitz way, not wanting to get her hopes up too much in her state, since I'm well aware that Moira has always been half in love with me. So, Charlene and Leila had wanted a masterful femme for discipline. I slicked my hands over my mullet, making it flop just so. Still dressed in my dishevelled femme drag, I thought I knew just the gal for the job.

En route down Mulberry Street, I gingerly patted my cheek, where the scratches still hadn't healed up. All you sex kittens out there, take a tip from Shifty Malloy: Gotta watch those nails. Me-*Ow*. All cats love fish but fear to wet their paws, or so the old saying goes, and that had been my experience too with Regina. But I had a surefire plan for Charlene and Leila. I'd get my pubes shaved in one of those Playboy bunny designs first. The act would give the girls even more of a treat before they went through the catflaps of yours truly.

And with that pretty thought in my head, I headed off down the pub to let Charlene and Leila know I'd found the purr-fect candidate. Oh, she might rabbit on a bit, but Ol' Shifty Malloy is a pussy girl at heart.

The Missionary Position

The Missionary Position

Ber-ring!

The doorbell blasted through my sweet dreams of candy softening on my lips, candy as vanilla as Marilyn Monroe, peppermint dissolving on my tongue, the taste of sugared pussy melting in my mouth. I lifted my head blearily to look at the alarm clock, then fell back on my pillow with fatigue and irritation and stared up at the ceiling. Eight o'fucking clock on a Saturday morning.

Ber-ring!

I shrugged on my bathrobe and ran my fingers though my short dreads. 'I'm coming, aren't I?' I growled out.

As I reached the hallway, the bell sounded again. You know, I thought, I am not going to be a happy bunny when I answer this door. I had had a long work-week, see, and until now this had been my only chance at a proper lie-in. Yes, chance would be a very fine thing.

I pulled open the front door and tried to glare and focus at the same time. 'Do you know what time it is?'

A chirpy bright-eyed girl of about twenty with pale-brown skin, neat cornrows and a blue blazer stood beaming at me. 'Good morning! I'm sorry to have woken you up so early, but I wondered if I could talk to you about religion for a min–'

'No.' I was already closing the door, but she stuck her foot in it, with more aggression than I had expected.

'Couldn't I come in for just a moment and show you some of our magazines? You never know, you might change your mind.'

I looked at her again, this time more closely. She was very pretty with ink-black eyes framed by long lashes, what looked like a curvy body under that horrible blue blazer and with a glow to her cheeks that had to be the result of religious fervour, I decided. The name-tag on her blazer read *Helena*.

'All right,' I said grudgingly. 'Come in, Helena.'

The girl followed me into the front room, commenting politely on my house. She liked it, she said. She admired what I'd done with the floorboards. Had I seen that technique on *Changing Rooms*?

'Tea?' I asked.

'Yes, please,' said the girl, and started to lay out reams of papers, religious pamphlets and magazines on the floor.

I returned and set her tea down on a side table. 'Here you go.' The girl looked slightly nervous – I wondered if she had noticed the bookshelf crammed with books, many of whose spines read in part 'Lesbian'.

'Do you want sugar with it?' I said softly, and moved very close to Helena. I could smell a musk coming up from her – fear or arousal, I couldn't tell. But it was sweet. Just like my dream had been.

'No,' murmured shy Helena, not raising her eyes to mine. 'No sugar.'

'Is something wrong?' I lifted her chin softly with my hand and innocently looked into her bright, dark eyes.

'No, no, there's not...' she demurred, and tried to look away, but I kept her chin in my hand.

'Maybe this?' I pressed my lips against her own lips and, to my surprise, she opened them and I was kissing deep into her wet, sweet mouth. My hand went beneath her blazer and ran over her crisp white shirt. 'Or this?' I undid the first two buttons, so that I

The Missionary Position

could now see the black lace bra sheathing her gorgeously full tits. 'Or even this?' I bent my head head to suckle at one nipple pressing through the lace, and could feel it swelling through the fabric.

God I must be horny, I thought, seducing a religious evangelist. Then again, it had been a hell of a dream. I was already wondering what her pussy would look like, smooth and juicy, already slick for the touch of my hands. As I thought this, Helena moaned and my hand inched up her pleated skirt to her thighs, and then rested on the plump curve of her arse. She wasn't wearing panties. Hmm. Missionary girl wasn't as pure as she presented herself to be. Hmm and hmm. She moaned again, and my hands shifted on her lush arse, trembled at its hole, and then moved to the wet cleft further on. Heaven.

Oh, god. My own clit was throbbing and I was wet myself. 'Oh, *god*,' I said it aloud and Helena nodded, no doubt mistaking the phrase for an invocation.

I slid my fingers into her lovely cunt and Helena sighed, and then I lowered her gently to the floor, on top of the confetti-spread of religious paper pamphlets. My fingers were working her pussy and now I twisted three of them deeper inside her and drove them in still harder, plunging into her wet sex. God, I was enjoying fucking this girl. I wanted to put my hand inside my robe and touch myself, too – I was so slippery – but I didn't want my attention to waver from the virtuous Helena, who was raising her hips up, raising her arse up so I could fuck her the way I wanted to: deep and fast.

She was tight around my fingers as she – almost coyly – snaked her hand down to rub her shiny little clit. It was so hot to see the little do-gooder wanking in my front room, her face so flushed I thought she'd burst, her lips very rosy as her tongue chafed at them, and her cunt tightening wet and firm around my fingers.

I wanted to touch myself badly, but I knew I couldn't stop.

'Christ!' Helena's pretty face screwed up as she came, and my hand was slick with her honey as she shouted the word. I was surprised by her blasphemy, but I continued pumping my hand into the hot liquid-velvet of her cunt until she motioned for me to stop and I was sure she'd finally had enough.

Yes, I was still aroused as Helena rose dazedly, pulled down her skirt, dusted off her blazer, murmured a quick thank-you and headed out the door.

Her tea hadn't been touched and was surely cold by now, I thought, as I leant back groggily on my sofa and looked over the array of slightly damp Christian pamphlets strewn over the floor of my front room. I wondered if she'd come back for them. I picked one up, and fumbled through a vitriolic discourse against homosexuality before tossing it in the bin near me. I had a feeling she'd soon be back again, and then I would receive my due satisfaction.

Conversions are not easy, you see, but the reward once a single soul's been saved is *always* worth the effort.

The Werfox

The Werfox

A bite, a snip, and Old Betsy was gone, just like that. For a fortnight after, the neighbourhood was more sullen than silent, and then folks started going about their business in the same manner as before. Things really hadn't changed too much. Elizabeth Marncell didn't push her granny cart down the pavement anymore. That was that.

And besides, there were other things in the neighbourhood to worry about. The two young men who'd moved into Flat 53 were suspiciously unrepentant and ineligible bachelors. One was called Jim (Mick Elphick's boy, from Upper Clapton) – he worked in advertising, and he was 30-ish, stocky and balding. He stretched his vowels on a by-way-of-Walthamstow rack and the result was friendly, Bob's-your-uncle, a half-pint, mate, thanks for asking. Because of his profession, you knew he'd sold his soul, but other than that, you couldn't pin a single fault on Jim Elphick, try as you might. No, the death of Elizabeth Marncell was probably not Jim's fault.

His boyfriend Craig was another matter. Craig was American, a mature student of computers, dull-looking and quite shy. He put up NOT-IN-MY-NAME anti-war posters in the street-facing window when it looked like Anthony Blair was jumping on the bandstand of the man (dubiously) elected president of Craig's homeland, *and* he always recycled the Hoegaarden bottles that the couple had delivered from Sainsbury's Online for only five quid, *and* he volunteered at two literacy projects, so the threatening qualities of Mr Craig Cane weren't immediately manifest. It was more a shade of the eye (grey); a slip of the tongue (he still omitted the 'h' in herbal after seven London years); a tone of the hair (rusty brown, and it is a proven fact that many Englishmen and women are groundlessly distrustful of ginger hair). The small things about a man that add up to and attest to his essential foreignness. No one on Mulberry Street, not even crazy old Moira Lagomort across the way, begrudged Jim his boyfriend. It was 2002, after all. It just would have been better altogether if Jim had settled down with a nice local boy.

If you walked by their house, you could look right in, because the young gents in question eschewed net curtains in favour of neo-yuppie wooden shutters that they always forgot to bind up. When the pensioner Trenton Bromley walked by one night, for example, he could see all the way through to the kitchen.

There stood Jim and Craig. They had their arms round each other's waist, and they were kissing ferociously. Then Craig-the-American moved his hands up to cup Jim's jaw, either side, and the kiss played on. You could make out the force of the kiss if you stood looking from the street, and you could see how Jim blushed but then recovered, and tried to put his hands everywhere on his lover – neck, ass, thighs, crotch, arms, fingers. Fingers. Jim licked, gently, Craig's thumb, with a subtle potency, and even through the window you could see Craig's lips part in a moan, and you could also imagine laughter from those exciting foreign lips.

Mr Bromley hurried into his adjacent flat and told his wife after dinner and after Brookside, so that the information wouldn't put her off her food.

That night the Bromleys both heard the moans quite clearly, though, through the wall that separated their flat from the

The Werfox

Cave-Elphick residence, as Jim sucked Craig's cock with a good deal more effort than he had his thumb, and Craig reciprocated in kind by curving his palm round Jim's cock and pulling him into a sugary state of sweat and sex and grip, faster and faster, until Jim shut his eyes and felt himself stretched elsewhere by Craig's broad sure hand, and felt the scratch-sweet twinges of unvarnished pleasure, little shocks like tiny icicles and wee fires, snippets of pain that flavoured the goodness of sex and made it still better, and he pulsed helplessly in Craig's fist, and felt quite the better for it.

As Craig and Jim lay blissfully in each other's arms, naked, happy, sleeping, Trenton and Tricia Bromley tossed and turned and couldn't drift off until 5.27 and 6.13 respectively, and then at 7.07 they were both wakened by the squawk of an ex-patriate Canada goose, right on schedule, that had recently begun performing morning solos of forty minutes minimum.

'Right,' said Tricia to her husband, 'this has got to stop.'

The *Hackney Mumble* later reported that four garbage cans had been overturned and two cats and one bird killed during the night, and that was when everyone on Mulberry Street knew a fox had come to town.

You need to remember that at this point emotions about foxes were running high all over England. The Countryside Alliance was gearing up for another march on London to support its favourite bloodsport of fox-hunting – not that people noticed that kind of thing too much in very civic surroundings of pavements and asphalt and street-cleaners (Londoners felt themselves more sophisticated and tolerant than barbaric hicks such as the CA), but all the same there was a measured sympathy for rural folk, since even city-dwellers remembered the foot and mouth crisis of the year before and the troubles of that slaughter. ('Though it's the sheep you felt sorry for, not the farmers,' commented Jim to Craig, as his thoughtful boyfriend served him breakfast in bed later that week.) So nearly immediately the Mulberry Street Fox Eradication Brigade was set up.

Some bad things happened.

A pigeon, a species over which no one normally concerned themselves much, locally referred to as the rat of the sky, with its throat torn out, lying in front of the Vietnamese takeaway one morning.

A compost heap belonging to a married City-attorney couple, totally destroyed.

A couple of boys in their early twenties who were swaggering along the street and had nothing better to do on a Saturday night threw rocks at Jim and Craig's shutterless windows, but they couldn't see in anyway too well since the sun-curtain was in place and it was still quite light outside but, if they had been able to, they would have seen Jim and Craig down on the floorboards together, sucking and fucking and laughing, coaxing kisses and come from each other, twined into a beast with two backs and two very prodigious horns. Their very Priapicity would make the hardest heterosexual man on earth flush, feel himself tightening and then excuse himself to the lavatory for a good five minutes at least.

One rock cracked through a lower pane, just a bit, and Jim replaced it fairly easily the next morning.

When Jim and Craig went out in the sunlight to trim the geraniums in the windowbox under the freshly replaced glass later that afternoon, they saw anti-fox posters plastered over the entire street – on every lamppost, tucked under the windshield wipers of every vehicle, half-flapping out of the mail-slots of every front door on Mulberry Street. 'They are a terrible menace,' the posters screamed, 'they stink and cause havoc to the order of a family garden; they destroy property and lives; they are a threat to our very way of life.'

They finished the replanting, swept the doorstep, and then

when they stepped back inside the house they latched up the wooden shutters across the main window. They remembered, for once. But light still came through in long skewers that touched the opposite wall, and when the two men reached for each other, the rays shifted on their bodies – a cheek, a shoulder, an elbow – and lit these patches for all the world like Jedi sabres, straight from the sun, pow.

Craig had a hand on top of Jim's head and rubbed the bristly short hair he found there, grinding it into his palm. He loved Jim so much. He loved him enough to stay in this dirty part of London. And when Jim nuzzled Craig's neck and ran a hand over the seat of Craig's jeans, pulling him into him, a sharp tremor started in Craig's crotch and rose all the way to his head. He felt dizzy with lust and crazy with love, as the sayings go. Their groins met, both cocks newly stiffened, and Craig put a hand down to feel the outline of Jim's rock-hard prick. He smoothed his palm over the extrusion, wanting to press it, keep it where it was and tease it. Their tongues were touching now, a light stimulation that only made the contrast of the heavy ache down below more piercing. Craig grabbed Jim even closer, making the light skip over the other man's skin, and when he pushed his fingers up under Jim's Armani shirt, he felt that when he finally removed it, Jim's whole body would reflect light, like a small stocky man-shaped moon, almost as if the wooden shutters weren't there and all the sun was coming in, all at once.

There were no new reports of fox activity during that night.

Craig ran into Mr Bromley in the garden the next afternoon and offered him some mint bunches, since he and Jim had grown too much, and Mr Bromley politely but stiffly declined. A man drove down the street in one of the cars that have both external speakers and built-in microphones, and shouted out that foxes were taking over the neighbourhood.

And that evening Craig and Jim were snubbed by Alice Trudy on the right, and Jim could have sworn that he heard Alice muttering about people with ginger hair, but he didn't want to report it back to Craig in case it made Craig feel like shit.

Instead he snogged Craig on the doorstep where everyone could see, and looked into his strange grey eyes and smiled.

That night Craig grew a tail, red and fluffy as the fur round a lady's fashion-coat. Yes, the analogy is meant to be ironic. Craig's teeth tapered out until he could bite a pigeon in half, or even an old woman who had spat at him and Jim, and then in the moonlight he looked down at his sleeping lover. Jim's eyes under his lashes moved as subtly as the breath that raised and lowered his torso, and Craig wondered what Jim's dreams were about, exactly. Craig caressed his own chest, ran a hand through the fine auburn pelt and then looked down again to see how vulnerable Jim's human body was – pale, nearly bald, loose in sleep. He would defend Jim tooth and claw. He loved the guy. The moon shafted through the Japanese-style bedroom blinds, and it wasn't nearly as strong as the sunlight had been the day before yesterday in the front room, not nearly as strong.

The next morning the *Hackney Mumble* ran a story stating that old Betsy Marncell hadn't been murdered bloodily after all, but had died of a fairly speedy aneurysm. They didn't know how they got the story so wrong the first time, and they were very sorry.

Mr Bromley leaned over the fence and told Jim that he had changed his mind and would take a bunch of mint after all if Jim and his, uh, young American chap didn't mind. Then Mr Bromley attempted a smile.

In No. 53, Jim and his grey-eyed boyfriend kissed, and Jim fingered animal skin, felt his tongue touch fangs, felt a claw tightening on his ass. They kissed more tightly. Then the impression faded. The room stunk of fox and sex and emergency, a wild sort of scent, and Jim wasn't sure he ever wanted it to fade tidily back into workaday domestic perfume. He nipped Craig's tongue unexpectedly and heard the other man growl softly with need.

Fox-hunting was eventually banned and the Countryside Alliance calmed down. The local Mulberry Street Fox Eradication Brigade never capitalised on the respectable attendance of its inaugural meeting, and the group slowly evolved to a Committee for Correct Disposal of Human Waste & Litter, a ponderous transition, almost like a beast losing hair and teeth, changing imperceptibly to a man. Tamed, you could even say.

Virgin Club

Virgin Club

I was darn proud of myself.

It takes a lot of stars to get your gold bar, you know. Five twinklers earn a star. Five stars earn a tenth of a silver bar. Five silver bars to get one gold one. That's a lot of twinklers: Honouring Thy Father and Mother, Being Aware of Constant Temptation, Reporting of Fellow Club Members Who Have Fallen From the Path, A Month of Masturbation-Free Days.

1,250 twinklers to get a gold bar.

Five demerits to lose them all in one fell swoop.

Ever since I joined Virgin Club, I've been high on Life. I've kept His face in front of me while I've been racking up my twinklers and after two years I've finally earned the gold bar, damn it.

Oops. Swearing: that's one demerit, at least. Promise me you won't tell Mrs Sister Stevens.

I could never get into the swing of the whole Drama Club thing – hello! It was full of geeks! – and I wasn't really good enough to be a cheerleader, and swim team just made my hair turn green. So when the President of the USA announced that his support for the Chastity Movement meant that there were going to be Virgin Clubs opening up in every state high school, well, I just jumped for joy. Because I was already qualified, see, not like some of those sl... some of those girls out there. I was sixteen when I signed up and I was still a virgin and proud of it. And when the Virgin Clubs became law two years later in January of this year, I was even prouder to know that I was doing it for God and Country.

See, now with that separation-of-church-and-state thing repealed and creationism the required curriculum in every secondary education system, our teachers can really get down to teaching us the Lord's work, not Satan's. They give us their full attention in Virgin Club; that's why there's only ever fourteen members – seven guys, seven girls – and one sponsor couple (married, naturally) per club. Why seven of each? Because that's how many days it took to create the good green earth. Virgin Club prides itself on creating men and women who believe in family values right from the start: Adam and Eve before they got a taste for sin.

I liked the songs best when I first joined Virgin Club: *'Oh, Say Can You See, It's Called Vir-gin-i-ty, We're Saved and It's Good, For It's Our Mai-den-hood!'* We used to put on our flag berets and just belt the words out, all us girls together, and then just LAUGH and LAUGH because it was so much darn fun being there together, giggling and hugging and blushing. We were doubly proud that as members of Virgin Club we got to wear the berets fashioned from Our Nation's Flag. Red for the blood of a wife offered up to her husband on her wedding night, white for her skin, blue for her eyes.

What do you mean, what kind of stuff do we do at Virgin Club? We do all kinds of things! Idle hands are the devil's work. We like to do stuff like hiking and chopping wood and cross-country running and shot-putting and really anything they think will, um, subliminate our desires. I think that's the word they use. Anything that will turn our minds to the holy temples of our bodies. They like to wear us out and that's just fine. I even like swimming now, because it's, what do you call it, invigorating. We girls always have fun fooling around in the showers, squirting each other with

Virgin Club

shampoo. We used to like to go boating too, until there was that environmentalist plot about the lake water being polluted, and a few of the commies still left in the Senate forced our blessed President to close the lakes for investigation, even though they were perfectly safe. Swimming, boating, canoeing, orienteering. Anything healthy and clean, that's what we like to do in Virgin Club.

We start each meeting by going down to the altar, where Mrs Sister Stevens and Mr Brother Stevens wait for us, because it's Confess-o-Rama time and you know what that means. Marissa Eggers told me that Confess-o-Rama was stolen from the Catholics, but she's a dirty liar and Mrs Sister Stevens and Mr Brother Stevens told me that wasn't the case at all. And Marissa Eggers got two whole demerits for lying and I got four twinklers for Reporting a Vicious Rumour, so ha ha ha. Mrs Sister Stevens and Mr Brother Stevens reminded me that I should feel sorry for Marissa, though, and look upon her with Christian forbearance. I have to try to be as good as they are. They are just, like, the most happily married couple I have ever seen. They are so cute.

Today at Confess-o-Rama it was William Light's turn first. He walked straight on up to the altar and he was already kind of crying by that point, and then he sneaked a look over to the half of the church where all us girls were sitting, and he said that he had been having impure thoughts about what boys and girls could do together, and then he even said the penis word, and we all gasped, and Mr Brother Stevens rushed William on out of the church right lickety-split. William ended up getting a demerit for Impure Thoughts and four twinklers for Honesty, we found out later.

When we left Virgin Club that night, though, guys out the left-hand door, girls out the right-hand one, we were all kind of buzzing from William's Confess-o-Rama, because what he said was SO scandalous. And Susan Seegan said that she had even seen a penis once; in fact, it was William's, and it had been all hard and stiff and she had felt it, and then we all shrieked at what Susan had said, but none of us ran back to Mrs Sister Stevens and told, even though we could have gotten a LOT of twinklers for it, because we thought if we were quiet then maybe Susan would tell us more. But she didn't and Marissa Eggers told her that she wouldn't last out the year as a virgin if she went on the way she was doing, and Susan shoved her, and we had to separate them, me and the other four girls, because they were really going at it, punching and pulling hair and kicking.

After me and Alison and Michelle and Toni and Penny stepped in and broke it up, they were both kind of huffing and puffing and Susan's face was all red.

'You're a slut,' Marissa told Susan.

But even though using bad language is easily a demerit, me and Alison and Toni and Penny and Michelle just kept our mouths shut and stared at them, wondering what was going to happen next. Because Susan was giving Marissa a LOOK.

Then, it got completely confusing, because Susan just put her arm around Marissa like they were best friends again and they kind of starting walking off together like nothing had happened and there had never been an argument about William at all.

Marissa put her head back over her shoulder and shouted back at me and Toni and Penny and Alison: 'Are you guys coming with us to the gym or not?'

See, the gym is where we like to go to work off all our excess energy and stuff. Mrs Sister Stevens says it's better than saltpetre.

Well, it was only six o'clock, because Club Night had ended early on account of William's Confess-o-Rama, so we all kind of looked at each other and then thought, why not? If our parents found out, we were only working out on the weights anyway. Or callisthenics and stuff like that. So the five of us dragged our heels after them, and Marissa and Susan kept up some distance ahead. I knew then that it was this kind of stuff I was going to miss when we all graduated in May and went on to Bible College or, if we were lucky, began dating a boy from Virgin Club under the supervision of Mrs Sister Stevens. I was going to miss this friendship stuff of us all being eighteen and all laughing and all being in a gang together, singing songs and wearing our berets, before the whole thing came to a halt in May and we had to go our separate ways. It made me kind of sad.

So I put my arm around Alison and she smiled up at me and I knew she was feeling exactly the same thing.

When we got to the gym I even started to have that buzzy feeling all over my skin, because not only did I know that we had more fun than anyone on earth, us girls in Virgin Club, but also I knew that we were keeping to the rules, because there wasn't a single boy present so we were doing just what Mrs Sister Stevens had taught us. So I guess that little buzz down between my legs when Alison hugged me real tight was virtuosity.

Here are the two rules of Virgin Club:

1) You shall not engage in any skin-to-skin contact nor contact of the clothing of a member of the opposite sex, including kissing and fondling, before matrimony. The week before your marriage you will consult and be advised by your sponsors regarding your wifely and husbandly duties.

2) Furthermore, you shall not flirt or talk inappropriately with members of the opposite sex, nor socialise with them, nor discuss the two rules of Virgin Club so as to tempt unduly.

None of us have broken the rules – not even Susan, despite what she said. Not one of us.

Astrid Fox

*

First thing, when we got inside the gym and it was all sweaty and hot, and the wrestling mats still smelled of the boys and their grunting and wrestling and sweating earlier in the day, but no one talked about that, because it might put impure thoughts about boys in our heads, and we all kind of try to support each other, not bring the others down, if you know what I mean, well, first thing Alison did once all seven of us were in there and the doors were shut, was she flopped herself on the sticky wrestling mat and kind of pulled her sweatshirt with the VC logo over her head.

'I'm really hot,' she said, 'Gosh darn it, but it's hot in here.'

And she was right, you know, because it *was* really hot and all of us were thinking the same thing, which was: that this was the kind of night that reminded us why we all liked Virgin Club so much.

So after Alison took off her sweatshirt, Toni, Michelle, Penny, Marissa, Susan and I followed suit, and we were all sitting there in our thin T-shirts, and I couldn't help noticing that everyone's nipples were kind of stiff and sticking out underneath the T-shirt fabric, even though it wasn't cold in the gymnasium at all. And then Alison leaned over and kissed me on the neck, and I felt sweet little tingles running all the way from my toes up to my scalp.

I forgot about everyone else in the room and just let Alison kiss me, her tongue wet and hot in my mouth, and I felt what Alison says is called my clit go stiff and my hole get wet. That little tingling feeling I'd had earlier had been revved up to a vibration as powerful as if I was sitting on top of my mom's washing machine at home. All I could think about was Alison's tongue, and where she might put it next. I grabbed out to her and started putting my hands all over her, pulling her on top of me. My palms were on her ass, then on her back, over the thin fabric of her T-shirt, then stroking her calves, feeling her slim muscles beneath her cargo pants. All of her flesh was as soft as one of those old-fashioned fake flowers of velvet and clotheswire you can buy at garage sales, as soft as that, except better, because there was life underneath my fingers. She was like organic velvet, moving and thrusting and wiggling. She was buzzing with life and she was making me buzz too. I thought then if she kissed me again, I might pass out, melt into all that softness like I was going to fall asleep for a thousand years.

She kissed me again.

Her tongue began to trace little circles down my neck, little paisley spirals of saliva, and she was sitting there in my lap, and my crotch was getting more and more of a burn, because although all this soft stuff was great, I just wanted her fingers in my pussy, as Alison calls it, my wet hot hole, and I could feel her wetness now too, her own crotch slippery with sap as she wiggled there on top of me, dripping through her panties. She was straddling me like a cowgirl.

'Get up, Canice,' she muttered, and I remembered how bossy Alison could be, and how pissed off she got when something didn't go her way. So I rose to my knees, immediately, as soon as she slid off me. She was standing over me, looking down at me all kind of flustered and red-faced and I knew that she was as excited as I was. All around us, I could kind of hear moaning and grunting and groaning, but I was only looking up into Alison's deep brown eyes, and it was kind of like all other sounds sort of had the volume turned down suddenly, because all I could hear was her voice, even though it was just a whisper, and she was saying, 'bend over, get over, bend over' over and over again like a kind of prayer.

When I thought of prayers, I thought about Virgin Club, and when I thought about Virgin Club I just praised God for being lucky enough to be a member, and being lucky enough to get Alison to kiss me everywhere, and to get Alison to use her fingers to dig down deep beneath my damp panties and touch me, stir me up until I was as wet as anything, and then run one long finger all the way up to my belly, and then further up, wiping herself on me so that when her finger hit my lips there was only a taste of me left, just a taste. The truth is, I wanted her *whole* hand down there inside me, fucking me hard (demerits don't count if you just *think* the bad words), a thumb on that rock-hard little bud of mine, slippery to the wrist with my, um, come. I wanted to be on my back shouting her name and God's too, in pure happy thanks.

But Alison never did exactly what I wanted, and I should have gotten used to this by now, because she still seemed determined to have me on my hands and knees, my skirt bunched up at my waist, my pantyhose and pale-pink nylon panties shoved down to my ankles but kind of holding me in place, like handcuffs I guess, so I couldn't move around a lot. So I did what I always did, which was what Alison wanted. It always turned out to be what I wanted too, eventually. I thought about how the pink nylon of my panties would show one long, damp, wet streak from all the juice that was slippery between my legs.

I was waiting there on all fours, and she hadn't touched me yet, and I was just pushing my ass towards her, yearning, wanting just a little feel from her. My hair was brushing the ground and I imagined what my ass would look like now, nearly in her face: big and smooth and still tan from my vacation in San Antonio three weeks ago when I wore a bikini all-day round, and I wiggled my ass just a little, just for her, and I knew how she would be able to see my cream oozing out from my pussy lips, and how she would be waiting to touch me. I could nearly smell myself. I had no idea how she was able to resist stroking me, one nice hot wet stroke, if you really want to know. I tried to concentrate on other things, because the anticipation was so intense it almost hurt. From somewhere across the sticky wrestling mats, I could hear Marissa groaning, too. Soon Alison would make me groan like that. I bit my lip and waited.

Alison took her time. And all the while I was repeating the

rules of Virgin Club like a chant in my head, and imagining each fuck-stroke of her hand in me: 'furthermore – you shall not flirt – or talk inappropriately – with members of the opposite –' and it was at this point that Alison put her hand in me at last, not soft or gentle, but fierce and fast, like she had been wanting to do nothing else, and had been thinking about touching me that whole long minute she waited, which I guess is pretty close to the truth, actually. And her fingers slid into me and I gasped and pushed my ass up against her hand, feeling totally degraded even though I knew I was virtuous and still stood – or kneeled, as the case might be – pure in the eyes of the Lord. 'Sex' – her hand sent shudders all the way up my gut, and I felt warm and so full I was going to split – 'nor socialise with them' – she got down on her knees too, and started to lick me as she fucked me, licked round my asshole, which I knew was dripping from all the cunt-juice that had been rubbed up from the action of her hand. Then she kind of slid herself underneath me like a car mechanic, I know it sounds crazy, but there she was under me while I grunted on all fours and bore down all over her hand, there she was fucking me with her hand nevertheless, and she just stuck out her tongue where her hand still was, drinking at my slit, swallowing my juice down. Her face must have been soaked, and she continued to fuck me the whole time, her mouth travelling over to my clit and sucking and giving it delicate little nips while she pumped me and pumped me with her hand, and I felt myself spill over her – 'nor discuss the two rules of Virgin Club' – and I began to jerk against her mouth; it felt delicious; it felt perfect; it felt heavenly, as in from heaven, and I was orgasming right there, on her mouth, on her hand, on her face – 'so as to tempt unduly.'

Alison kind of scooted herself out from underneath me then and I stayed there on my hands and knees, continuing to tremble, and I watched while she shoved a hand down underneath her panties and rubbed herself as hard as she could, leaned back and just gave into herself, eyes screwed up, one hand between her legs, one underneath her T-shirt pinching at her nipple as rough as she could, grunting and rubbing hard against her own hand until she was going at it like a jackhammer, and then she came, I guess. This had the effect of making me turned on all over again, but I stayed in position 'cause Alison hadn't technically given me permission to move and, believe me, I've learned the nice way to do what Alison says. I wanted to touch myself, 'cause I had that buzzing, burning feeling between my legs, but I tried to pay attention to what Alison was saying, because she had managed to get herself up off the floor and was whispering in my ear now, saying, 'Listen, listen.'

And I stopped to listen then, and I could hear that sound I had heard before, which was that moaning-groaning-moving, and it was like the whole gymnasium with its sticky mats was echoing, and so then Alison said 'Get up, you can get up now,' and so I did get up. I looked across the gymnasium: there were Susan and Marissa, crumpled into each other, French-kissing and playing with each other's hair with sticky fingers. The sound wasn't coming from them. There were Toni, Penny and Michelle, fingers still in each other's cunts, linked like one of those Add-A-Pearl necklaces you fasten together, but obviously finished with their fun because they were talking and laughing softly, and the sound wasn't coming from them, not anymore.

So Alison kind of shuffle-shoved me over to the door that led out from the gymnasium to the room with the window that looked out over the weightroom, and I let her, and Toni and Penny and Michelle and Susan and Marissa all followed suit, and pretty soon we were all there looking at Scott Phillips and Dean Lear down in the weightroom, and we stood there all girls together, Alison's arm tight around my shoulder and feeling pretty good, and we watched as Dean Lear had the stiff hard thing between his legs sucked by Scott, and Dean had got his eyes closed and he was

Virgin Club

lying back down on the bench press and he didn't even know we were watching, all of us girls. He just let Scott swallow him down, licking at him like he was a lollipop or maybe something even better, like an ice cream cone or pure frozen Cool Whip on a ice-cold spoon in hot summer.

The relief we felt was something else, I tell you, because imagine if they had been in there with girls! I mean, we'd have to tell, wouldn't we, because that's just the sort of thing we'd have to report, and Scott and Dean would have been thrown right out of Virgin Club if they'd broken the first rule, that's for *sure*. Me and Marissa and Penny and Michelle and Susan and Toni and lovely Alison with her arm round me, we sure were relieved to see it was just all boys together, down in the weightroom.

I mean, it's Virgin Club, isn't it? And we're all of us, boys and girls, keeping ourselves pure from the taint of the opposite sex and the lustful desires that proximity inspires, and keeping ourselves pure *for* the opposite sex, too. So on our respective wedding days, we'll all be able to say, hands on hearts, we were married as virgin men and virgin women. Because that's what Virgin Club is all about.

Honest to God.

New erotic fiction from Red Hot Diva

Cherry
Charlotte Cooper

It's sexy. It's sassy. It's so, so slutty.

Desperate to pop her lesbian cherry, Ramona soon finds that shagging women in real life bears little resemblance to the dirty books she's been reading under the covers. Every dyke has to ditch the theory and put herself out there if she wants to get some action and *Cherry* goes all the way... Ramona pursues and is pursued by the coolest, hottest, richest, wildest – and sometimes the saddest – girls around.

"Modern, mucky, memorable, masturbatory dirt that delivers. As Ramona would say: Lap it up!" **Babe / Rockbitch**

"Rollicking good fun... one of the naughtiest, dirtiest, smuttiest erotic novels we've ever had the pleasure to read" **Rainbow Network**

"Every variety and permutation of sex you could think of, and a few you probably couldn't... chock-a-block with relentless lurid sex" **Time Out**

"Harder edged than 'Sex and the City', real sex as opposed to posing with sheets. Lesbian adolescence has never been so much fun" **What's On UK** [Also book of the month!]

RRP £8.99 UK/ $13.95 US
ISBN 1-873741-73-1

Scarlet Thirst
Crin Claxton

Lesbian vampires on the prowl!

Sexy Rani is initiated into the vampire lifestyle by the butch dyke Rob and embarks on a hedonistic trip through a sex-fuelled underworld, seducing and being seduced by more and more women who live the Life...

For once, the lesbian vampire story is not just a metaphor: this novel is as upfront about sex as it is about biting into beautiful young necks.

They're butch, they're femme, they're out for blood.

'A fangtastic read for fans of Buffy, Willow and Tara!' Gay Voice

RRP £8.99 UK/ $13.95 US
ISBN 1-873741-74-X

How to order your new Red Hot Diva books

Red Hot Diva books are available from bookshops including Borders, Libertas!, Silver Moon at Foyles, Gay's the Word and Prowler Stores, or direct from Diva's mail order service on the net at www.divamag.co.uk or on freephone 0800 45 45 66 (international: +44 20 8340 8644).

Please add P&P (single item £1.75, two or more £3.45, all overseas £5) and quote the following codes: Scarlet Thirst SCA74X, The Fox Tales FOX790, Cherry CHE731.